Broken

M.A. McNally

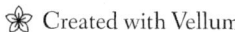 Created with Vellum

For Andy, Charley, Heidi, Cam, Steven & Max

CONTENT GUIDANCE:

This novel explores aspects of domestic abuse and mental health and contains depictions of self-harm, alcohol abuse, animal cruelty, blood and gore, child abuse. Please read with care.

Part One

Jesse

Chapter One

"If you never heal from what hurt you, you'll bleed on people who didn't cut you."

— Unknown

1st May 1985—age nine

I can hear the scary music. She's playing it again. Please God, make her and her music die.

I know she's in one of her dark moods. I'm scared.

I didn't mean to ask her to die, it just came into my brain. If I take it back, will you stop her from coming to get me?

Dropping to my knees, concentrating hard, saying the words over and over just in case God hasn't heard me above all the other children praying tonight, the music gets louder.

"Please God, I'm sorry. Please don't let her come and get me. I promise to be good. Please don't let her come and get me again."

I think my mother has heard me.

"Jesse, you little bitch. I'd better not find you hiding again."

Scrambling up onto the bed, rocking back and forth, praying. I don't think God can hear me. Mother tells me God hears everyone. The nuns at school tell me God hears everyone. Why can't He hear me now?

A cupboard slams making me jump. Quickly looking towards the door, I hear a bottle being opened and a glass filling with what is probably whisky. A match is struck.

Eyes glued to the door, the smell of the incense soon floats up the hall and under my door.

Swallowing hard, I feel sick.

Crossing myself again, hoping God can smell it too, is He coming to help me? He's never stopped her yet. Tonight might be different.

Waiting.

My heart's changed places with my brain; I can't even hear the music, there's a huge drum – inside my body – thumping.

Slipping the blankets over me, covering my ears with my hands, rocking in the dark, in time with the drum, I hum a song in my head and try to pretend what's coming is good and not bad.

It's too late.

Thump, thump, thump.

Thundering down the hall like a stampede of elephants; I wish they were coming to stamp on her and not me.

Frozen like a statue underneath my blankets, she bangs through the door.

"Where are you, you little bitch?"

Stomping to me, my blankets are ripped off, I'm cold, quickly putting my arms above my head, peeking through my fingers at her sneery ugly face. Hand above her head ready to hit me, I know what will happen if I don't lower my arms.

"Please don't. I'll be a good girl, I promise. Please, Mother, please?"

Yanking me up by the wrists like I'm made of air and glueing me to her hip. I kick her stomach to get away.

She doesn't feel a thing.

Punching her as hard as I can with my legs and arms as she walks slowly past a picture of God smiling, I try to grab it, but my arms are too short.

Why isn't He helping me?

I feel sick.

The smell of whisky, cigarettes, and the incense she burns is getting stronger. Stumbling, steadying herself on the kitchen door-frame, a half empty bottle of whisky on the table nearly falls.

I know why she can't walk properly.

Dropping me on the cold tiles, my bruises-on-bruises sting, but I don't cry. Pushing myself up, standing in the middle of the kitchen, glaring at her.

I won't let my eyes show her how much I'm hurting.

"Take your pyjamas off."

Why does she want me to undress? She's never done this before.

"No."

Ripping my pyjama top over my head. "Off with your bottoms," she screeches.

Why didn't I hide in a wardrobe, sneak out the back door? Find somewhere safe?

Whack.

Lowering my pyjama bottoms to the floor, the cold claims me, shivering like a chicken that's just been plucked.

"Get on the chair. Now."

Doing as I'm told; she ties me to the chair cutting into my flesh with the string. The holy water on the table in the shape of Our Lady prays for me.

No. Please God, don't let her do it again. Help me God. Please? Help me.

Chapter Two

"The growth is not in letting go of something or someone that is toxic. It's in letting go of THE PART WITHIN YOURSELF that feels like you need them in the first place."

— Jovanny Ferreyra

12th January 1996 — eleven years later

Republica. Who doesn't love them? I love all their songs except one. It reminds me of the hell I'm in. The problem is, I love the beat and really wish the lyrics were different.

Staring out of my window, 'Out of the Darkness,' the song in question, blasts out of my speakers behind me, looking and listening for any signs of my boyfriend Jayden's motorbike. He's due home any minute, if I'm not properly ready for when he gets here he'll be angry. The first thing he'll check is whether I'm wearing the stupid outfit he left out for me to wear. They're definitely getting worse, probably because the porn he's watching is getting worse, or he's bored with me.

Who knows?

I wish he'd have a freak accident on his bike or die unexpectedly, but I wouldn't be that lucky. He'd come back to life and hunt me down for sure.

He wasn't like this in the beginning. I actually liked him and thought I'd faint from just looking at him.

He took me to the movies, bought me dinner and sent me love cards just because. I felt like the only girl in the world.

In the blink of an eye he changed. He turned ugly and mean. Not just a little mean, but really fucking mean.

Possessive, controlling, abusive, I'm now locked in the flat whenever he goes out. I'm only letting him do it to stop him thinking I'm sneaking anyone in. I'd rather give in to his paranoia than have to explain away something I haven't even done.

All my friends have gone, even Lola. I thought she'd stay with me for life. I thought she'd be my best friend forever, but she, as well as everybody else, were fed up with Jayden flipping out and losing his shit if they said or did anything he didn't like.

Celeste, an old workmate of mine, hates him. She visited us once after going to see the latest Mel Gibson film and innocently told me to go see it because of Mel's cute butt scene in the shower.

How was she to know what would happen because of that one remark?

Jayden's eyes had already turned and there was nothing I could do. When she left, he dragged me to the video store, picked up some movies and watched them the rest of the day while I was made to lay in bed next to him with a sheet over my head. I didn't move until he was 'ready' for me. He beat me twice that night and banned me from seeing or talking to Celeste ever again, even at work.

I miss her.

I don't really understand why I keep putting up with all his shit.

I suppose when I realised there was something horribly wrong, it was too late. I was hooked and all the people I loved were gone, except my beautiful cat Samantha.

He let me keep her.

Seeing my reflection in the window, I suppose I deserve my lot. I know things have to change, that I have to stand up to him one day. I'm too scared, though. I'm scared of everything.

If I was still living at The Orchard, my old place of work, I'd be safe. Even though it's a brothel and some of the men were a bit dodgy, I always felt protected, safe. When Jayden found out I worked there he put a stop to it straight away, pretty sure the reason he asked me to steal money from the till was so that Sharon would eventually find out and sack me. I think it was his plan all along.

I miss Sharon, my old boss. She's the grandmother I always wanted and never had. I'll regret hurting her for the rest of my life. The disappointment on her face when she found out it was me stealing the money. I'll never forget it. I had to leave and never step foot back in the place. I miss it so much.

I shouldn't have done what I did.

Grabbing my bottle of vodka off my side table, I pour myself another one, placing it down, wiping smoke stains from the window, still listening for Jayden's motorbike. A car suddenly screeches outside stopping in the middle of the street.

An old man runs out onto the road to pick up a little boy who's nearly been hit by a car. He looks angry, like he wants to smack the boy who's screaming, but I doubt he wants to hurt him by the way he's hugging him close to his chest. Picking him up carefully, taking hold of his little hand, he gently brushes the hair from his eyes and leads him onto the pavement where lots of people are there to check on them.

A tiny woman with long brown hair dressed in nothing but black stops to ask if the boy is okay. The heavy black sunglasses she's wearing are far too big for her face and make her look like a movie star. Is she? The old man's smiling at her, looking a bit confused. I'm guessing he's wondering who she is or why she's wearing black in the sun. Stupid woman. She'll bloody roast.

A teenage girl in the skimpiest green and pink shorts and matching tank top runs past with headphones attached to her Walkman. She hasn't seen a thing.

I bet Jayden would love her.

He'd love her young, pretty, sexy flesh.

I *hate* her.

Banging the window with my fist, screaming at her from above, others look up to see what the noise is, ducking behind the curtain, sipping my vodka, watching until they lose interest.

I love to people watch. It gives me something else to concentrate on, not that it helps much. My thoughts always come back to Jayden. Nearly dropping my glass, catching it quickly; buses, trucks, cars, and cyclists' whizz past as the lights change from green to orange to red. A particularly noisy bus struggles under the weight of its passengers, the chug-chug of the exhaust gasping for breath under its heavy load.

A mother and child sit at the front, both staring into space at the traffic out the window, not a single word uttered between themselves. The boy looks sad, like his little face is on the verge of tears. What has the mother done to him?

The bitch.

Whirring, the washing machine distracts me, signalling it will end its cycle soon. A gentle meow from the kitchen door reminds me I'm not alone.

My beautiful Samantha needs feeding.

Beep. Beep. Beep.

"*Piss off*, you stupid bloody washing machine."

Grabbing the bottle of vodka from my side table, I top up my glass and gulp it back in one, my third in an hour.

Not overly busy for a Thursday afternoon, nobody says hello or even smiles as they pass each other, all going about their business totally oblivious to me watching them from above.

A large old lady in a long brown dress and matching scarf bends, struggling to walk under her weight. Suddenly she turns, stands, and looks straight up at me. Yelling at her, she doesn't hear me.

"Look at me, old lady. Can you see me?"

Willing her to see me, waiting for our eyes to connect, there's nothing.

"*Fuck you*. Fuck off and die then, you old bitch."

Why didn't she see me?

Looking away from the window to the mirror, I wish my reflection was someone else, someone happy. If Jayden left the door unlocked, it would at least feel less like living in a prison. I really don't understand why he does it. He says it to protect me and that he'll only be an hour, but that always turns into three, four, five. What the fuck does he think would happen if there was a fire?

I tried running once when the door was unlocked. That hadn't ended well. I'd spent days recovering, and afterwards, Jayden made sure to put two locks on the door just in case it happened again.

One day I'll have the guts to go, get out. I won't let him do this to me forever.

My picture of Jesus above my mirror stares at me with eyes as blank as mine. I still don't know why I bought it. It comforts me in a weird way. I shouldn't want any reminders of my homelife growing up, but just seeing Him makes me feel safe, protected if anything should happen to me.

God will never want you.

My mother's voice is always there, in the background.

I wish Jesus would protect me from her words.

One day I'll be free. One day her voice won't be there anymore.

Closing my eyes, soaking up all the noises around me, pretending I'm somewhere no one can control me or my thoughts, there's just me and my beautiful silver tabby; happy and free.

Honk.

A car screeches.

"Fuck off."

The multi-coloured clock made out of spoons says it's three o'clock. Sitting on the wall next to the kitchen, it's such a stupid clock, throwing the first thing I can find at it. Sticking, hanging from the long hand, I'm amazed the slipper has landed. I hope it breaks it.

Swallowing, my throat feels like gravel inside.

"Just one more for the road?"

Pouring another shot straight into my glass, I don't give a fuck. Seeing a joint in the ashtray and lighting it, I don't give a fuck.

Trying to find my black eyeliner amongst all the shit on my vanity top is like looking for a needle in a haystack. My mind and hands aren't in sync, which isn't helped by the booze and weed. I don't really want to find my eyeliner. What I want is to lay down on my bed with Samantha and sleep for a zillion years. I want my brain, eyes, and hands to look for anything other than the black eyeliner but I find it underneath a cloth.

Fuck.

Eyeliner in hand, staring at myself, my eyes look dull, deflated, dead.

Even when I lived with my monster mother I was happier than this. At least I could guess what was going to happen from one day to the next. Jayden turns into Jekyll in the blink of an eye and there's nothing I can do but wait until he changes back.

Steadying my elbows, swigging my vodka straight from the bottle, shivering from the taste, my body doesn't want me to drink anymore but I ignore it, tracing a black line over the bright-blue eyeshadow I already have on. I look stupid, comical, and now the pencil is smudged down the side of my right cheek because of my shaky hands and it's mixed with my overdone rouge.

Black tears race each other down my face to my chin; dabbing them with anything I can find.

"You stupid bitch. How bloody ridiculous do you look?"

Pointing my pencil, singing along at the top of my voice – '*Don't You Ever*' plays in the background – not caring if anyone can hear.

This is one of my favourite albums; pretty sure I know every word to every song, even the one with the shit lyrics.

Tapping my pencil in time to the music, singing into the mirror, using it as a microphone, I'm Saffron, the lead singer, bold, beautiful, and ballsy. Pouring some vodka into my glass, standing, dancing, singing, spilling my vodka, picking up my joint, inhaling, coughing, nearly falling over, steadying myself on the corner of the dressing table, I sit back on my stool and watch the ceiling spin in time to the music.

Weeeeeee.

Dropping my glass, it joins all the ashtrays, G-strings, more glasses, make-up, and crap everywhere; finding the closest ashtray to stub out my joint.

Why am I being so careful? I'll die one day. Why not make it today?

Staring into the mirror, listening to Saffron singing in the background, the yellow bruising around my right eye is fading; very different to a beating eight months earlier when the white of my eye was completely red.

The night that happened I thought I was going to die. I couldn't move out of bed for days; sure Jayden had knocked my brain against my skull. I'm convinced the migraines that had started straight after were because of it. I'd vomited into a bucket for three days; poor Sharon had rung for a week thinking I was dead.

I loved her for that.

Tracing the fading bruising from a recent beating with my finger, I remember how it all started. A simple slap across my cheek for daring to open the door to our rented room without Jayden's permission.

Why did I ever lay eyes on him? I should've run the first time it happened. I should never have gone back.

Chapter Three

"Remember this. Because it will happen many times in your life.
When people show you who they are the first time, believe them.
Not the 29th time."

— Maya Angelou

Wednesday the 6th of March—two years ago

"It's retro night, ladies."

Joni, the gorgeous Fijian doorman welcomes us in his best Miami Vice voice.

"We know," saying in unison, excited for the night ahead.

Lola, my best friend, who loves dressing up for themed nights, has gone all out and worn next to nothing in a low-cut yellow leotard Olivia Newton John would never have worn. Removing her white shaggy coat, flashing some flesh, everyone's watching, except Joni, who just looks bored.

I'm with him.

I don't care or want anyone's attention.

Wearing black most of the time, I usually cover everything up, except tonight. I've let Lola talk me into wearing one of her black crop-tops and already I'm uncomfortable. I don't know why I agreed. It's not like anyone's going to look at me over her. She'd have a heart attack on the spot if that ever happened. Unsuccessfully trying to cover my flesh, I turn my attention to Joni.

"You're looking very Rrrrrrico tonight."

Winking, rolling my r's – it's a lot harder than I think – lingering ever so quickly over his perfectly proportioned biceps and thighs bulging through his Miami Vice get up. He's very cute, giving Tubbs a run for his money. Joni's lovely but I don't fancy him. It doesn't mean I can't admire what I see, though.

I'm more attracted to a bad boy.

Not a really bad, bad boy, just the same as in all the films. They always come good in the end and seem more interesting, more fun than the geeky good guys. The geeky ones never have the same allure, and anyway, I'd already fallen in love with a geek and it hadn't ended well. Lola had made sure of that.

Joni, I would say, is a cross between the two. He's definitely got the look of a bad boy, but he's a bit of a geek, too. I can be myself around him, which is rare for me, especially where men are concerned. I feel he's looking after me, like a brother with a sister. The first time he threw some drunk man out for being a bit too leery with me in the queue I knew he had my back. Joni came out of nowhere, grabbed the guy and threw him across the street quicker than the speed of light. I never thought he had it in him. He's usually so mild and gentle mannered.

Cheeks bright pink, clicking us both in, Lola punches his shoulder, one of her long pink fingernails piercing right through his shirt to his skin underneath. Lips snarled; growling aggressively at Joni; her furrowed eyebrows leave no question as to what she'd like to be doing to him. Not having any of it, Joni's look warns her off, flinching her hand away aggressively. I've never seen him like this before. He defi-nitely doesn't like her.

Bending down and whispering in my ear, he asks, "How can you two even be friends?"

Answering with my shoulders, walking the twenty steps up to the club with Lola, I turn to wave at him but he's shaking his head looking confused. I know he likes me, but he's definitely got it in for Lola, pretty sure the feeling is mutual. I don't know why, which confuses me. Lola thought he was gorgeous the first time she met him. As far as I know nothing's happened. Or has it?

As Lola gives him the bird from the top of the steps, he ignores her, instead checking out the hole she's left in his shirt. Glaring up as she opens the door to the club, he clicks two more people in yet more Olivia Newton John costumes in. Lola hasn't seen a thing.

"I see your friend's still a prick, Jesse. I'm not surprised."

Boom.

Stepping through the door, feeling the vibrations from the huge speakers through the floor, we're nearly blasted back down the stairs, covering our ears with both hands as we shake in time to the heavy bass.

Standing in line, waiting to be welcomed by the owner, Rick the slick, Ricki for short, the opening riff to one of my favourite songs comes on, nudging Lola to start dancing with me. Sneering at me like I'm a total embarrassment, I stop.

How can she not know '*Sex I'm a...*' by *Berlin?* It's so risqué and rude.

People's reactions are mixed. Some start dancing about for joy like me, and others stand looking at each other wondering what the hell the DJ is playing now?

Lola, of course, is one of the latter.

"What the hell is this crap?"

She clearly doesn't listen to the same music as me.

Happy about the DJ's choice of song – I'd only mentioned it to him a few weeks back – glad he's added it to his excellent repertoire of music. Singing along to make my point, Lola laughs a little too much, eyebrow arched in question, lip curled up into a smirk.

"If you're a slut then I'm fricking Mother Teresa."

Bursting into fits of laughter, waiting to be greeted on a not so usual Wednesday night, DevO's, a little club in the heart of Wellington, where we always end up on our joint night off, is buzzing.

Reunited for eight months now, our friendship is well and truly back on track... just.

Lola couldn't help herself. She'd deliberately ruined any chance I had with Jim, my first real crush. I'd forgiven her, but it didn't mean I still didn't fucking hate her for doing it. It had well and truly reminded me just how horrible she could be and how she'd stop at nothing to get what she wanted.

Even our friendship.

In her brain, the last two years and eight months hadn't happened and she just expected for us to resume our childhood positions. If I'm honest, I slid right back into it.

She has a way of getting away with it. I should know, if Lola wants anything, Lola gets it regardless of who she hurts.

After being flung out of home by my mother ten days before my sixteenth birthday, I thought I'd never see Lola again. I didn't think I'd survive one day let alone two years without her, especially as I'd had to live on the streets for weeks with no way of letting her know where I was. If I'd known where she lived I could've gone there, but in the whole time we'd been friends, she'd never invited me to her house. Not even once.

Thank God I met Gail, a woman who'd been on the streets for most of her life. I probably would've ended up in a body bag if she hadn't taken me in and taught me everything I needed to survive. She'd even let me live with her and then helped me get my job and place to live at The Orchard, a brothel her best friend Sharon still owns. Gail turned out to be more than my saviour. The night before she died I discovered she was my aunt. My mother had never told me about having a sister, ever.

I wear a necklace Gail gave me every day to remind me of her, my aunt I never knew I had.

Making friends with some of the girls at The Orchard, I actually started to enjoy life without Lola.

I used humour to mask a lot. None of the girls would've guessed my childhood had been so awful.

But, one night a monster from my past walked into The Orchard and I freaked wanting Lola with me. I missed her. I always felt a part of me was missing and thought she'd be feeling the same way too, so on her eighteenth birthday, I went looking for her.

When we reconnected I presumed she'd be different, that the long separation would've changed her.

Nothing's changed.

She's still the boss, and has taken off from where she left off like the entitled princess she is. I, of course, have complied without even batting an eyelid.

I'm used to it.

If I'm honest, it's a lot easier to just give in and avoid all the drama that comes with her not getting her way. Everyone her whole life has done it, including her parents.

Recently she's told me she was adopted, something that nearly killed her. She found out the same night I was flung out of home which made me sad because I wasn't there to support her.

I imagine her whole world turned upside down that night. I know how tired of her parents she was, but I don't think for one minute she ever wanted to be adopted.

Louise, her adopted mother, has always been jealous of the attention Lola gets. From what she's told me about her mother, I'm not surprised to hear Louise saved that little bomb for her sixteenth birthday.

I've often wondered if Lola's real mother would've been the same?

Samantha hates Lola. I think she's hated her from the first day they met. Scratching and hissing one time too many, Lola ignores her now, which suits everyone fine. In fact, I think she's a little scared of my silver feline, which cracks me up. Lola's never been scared of anything.

Back for what feels like ages, she's taken charge of not only my favourite hangout joint, but my workplace too. Eight months later, she practically runs the show. What's worse? Sharon allows it because she earns four times as much money as any other girl, which Lola never lets anyone forget. The other girls avoid her like the plague, making excuse after excuse not to socialise if they think she'll be there. They do as they're told, though. Everyone does for an easier life where she's concerned.

What Lola wants, Lola gets.

Always has, always will.

It's suffocating working together, so it's good to get out and have some fun somewhere else.

Not that I have much fun.

I usually just watch her collect more and more admirer's week after week.

It's fine by me. I'm happy to catch up with Joni and Greg the DJ and listen to the music, the one thing in my life that has never let me down.

"Sex, oh yeah you know you want me."

Sneering, Lola's hand tells me to stop.

"Freak."

Ricki welcomes us as he does all his customers, with a kiss on both cheeks. Milli Vanilli starts to sing from the speakers as he shoves me aside to focus on Lola and her cleavage. Let the circus commence.

Nudging his arm hard, his girlfriend reminds him she is there, watching, obviously not happy with the attention he's giving Lola.

Very handsome for his age, I've always thought Ricki looks much younger than his fifty-four years. Tall and lean with olive skin and hair dyed pitch-black and greased into a perfect 1950's quiff like Elvis, his dark, brooding, brown eyes smile; cheeky deep dents in both his cheeks and pointy chin perfectly show off his chiselled jaw. A gleaming white smile grabs the attention of women of all ages, including his current girlfriend, Cyndy, who, younger than him by twenty-eight years, stands to his left.

Legs up to her neck, scrawny and hollow, they're barely able to hold her or her wild blonde hair piled high on top of her head up. Bones to make a skeleton jealous, she's nervous.

Everyone's nervous around Lola.

Narrow red lips broken into a forced grin show off deep lines around her mouth, probably from smoking too many cigarettes. Small, hooded, round, brown eyes thick with black eyeliner and mascara, look even smaller with the makeup; her sharp pointy thin nose, pronounced cheekbones and ever so slightly lined, square-shaped face, make you assume she is nearer Ricki's age than her own. Handsome rather than pretty, I'm sure women as well as men find her their type.

A sizable mole in the middle of her forehead is the only real unattractive feature, peering down like a third eye while the club lights hit it on and off.

Snorting with laughter, Lola starts to point at it, but I won't let her tease Cyndy, quickly guiding her finger to the black, skin-tight, leather pants Cyndy has on instead.

Nudging me in the ribs, glaring, she's not so beautiful when she's being a bitch.

"Oi, you freak. You were going to laugh at it, too."

"Ouch, you bitch, and no, I wasn't. That's not nice, Lola. She can't help looking like that."

"Whatever. Who do you think she's trying to pull off? Cyclops gone rogue?"

Watching Cyndy tell Ricki off, the black trousers, black off-the-shoulder top and open-toe black high heels don't look anything out of the ordinary until you see the black T-birds jacket draped over one shoulder, giving away her retro inspiration for the night.

Lola goes in for the kill.

"Olivia Newton John? Well, well, seems like we both had the same idea. Which one do you like best, Ricki?"

Tiny slits glare, signalling to Lola to back off and even though she knows Cyndy's uncomfortable, she thrusts her chest forward challenging her to a silent duel. Both eyes fixed on each other like cats ready to pounce, I'm quite excited to see which one cracks first.

"Now ladies, there's enough of me for the both of you."

Ricki comes to the rescue lapping up the attention like a puppy.

Playfully slapping his shoulder, I can tell Lola's not comfortable with his attention by the way she answers.

"Ricki, you dirty devil, you could be my father."

It's the same every time we come. Cyndy hates Lola for being so perfect and Ricki loves her for being just that.

I'm so fed up with having to watch it.

Why can't they just all get on like normal people?

Placing a poker chip in each of our hands, Ricki's perfectly manicured hand points to the bar.

"Go order yourselves a free drink, ladies, and Lola? Here's another one for you."

Dropping my chip, quickly squatting to the floor to pick it up, I have to cover both ears with my hands because Greg's speakers have blasted throughout the club causing everyone to groan in protest. Ricki, in the middle of kissing Lola's palm, angrily turns towards Greg with slitted eyes, turning back to Lola, bringing his lips to her cheek; slyly inserting his tongue into her right ear. Everyone can guess where he'd like his tongue to be, watching him staring into her eyes with dirty old man lust. Yanking her away from his leery face, he follows her ass towards the bar, licking his lips, making me a little bit sick in the mouth, him seeing me, quickly turning back to Cyndy whose icy stare dares him to keep looking.

Standing, overlooking the dancefloor, leaning on the rails playing with our poker chips, I can't help myself.

"Why do you let him touch you up like that? Don't you think it's a bit creepy? And what the hell has Joni done that you hate him so much?"

Following Lola's gaze to where Ricki stands, her smirk tells me all I need to know. Lips curled up, eyes smiling, she doesn't mind the attention. In fact I think she gets some sort of kick out of playing with Cyndy who clearly feels uncomfortable and insecure around her. Laughing out loud, she ignores my questions pointing to the dance floor.

"Not as creepy as some of these outfits. Look at them."

She's right.

Tutus and leg warmers all different shades of neon-pink, electric-blue, yellow, and orange cover waists and legs of all different shapes and sizes. Dungarees paired with crop-tops not dissimilar to mine, makes me conscious I'm wearing one, pulling mine down over my tummy. Big hair teased to an inch of its life coupled with Dr Marten boots the same as mine, scream Bananarama. Very cool. There are so many Boy George lookalikes it makes anyone think he was the only original male icon of the 80's.

There were so many more.

Two men wearing false dreads sing to each other, one turning to expose his bare bum, the other clapping his hands together, slapping it hard.

Laughing, eyebrows arched in unison, Lola, and I look at each other both knowing what we're going to say.

"Gross."

Eyeing up all the women in leotards, I think Lola's happy none of them look as good as her.

"Look at the leotards. Bloody awful. I'd better go down and show them how it's done."

She isn't wrong.

It seems they all think they have bodies as good as Olivia Newton

John, the amount of flesh on show is anything but, as stomachs, bloated from alcohol, and thighs so dimpled it takes a second for the flesh to keep up with the dance moves, wobble all over the floor like a sea of jelly. I kind of like their confidence, wishing I was half as fabulous as them.

"I think they look pretty cool, and they're not short of attention by the looks of it?"

Crowds of men gathering around them vie for their attention. Full of confidence, I wish I was like them.

Lola will soon put a stop to it.

I already feel sorry for them.

"Let's have a drink before you piss anyone off with your perfect body."

"Bloody freaks. I'll have the usual."

Handing me her chips and walking to secure a table she's spotted in the back, men's eyes follow her every step, making their way to her like bees to honey.

Spotting my reflection through a mirror, my clothing choice clashes badly with the bright colour's others are wearing. The usual short, black tube-skirt I'm wearing clings to my size fourteen thighs a little too snugly and my black crop-top, pulling it down over my midriff, just hides my full bosom from wandering eyes. My abs aren't as tight as I'd like them to be, but I suppose they're not too bad either, taking a glance around the place comparing mine to others on show. Pulling my top down to cover my tummy, it won't stretch, leaving my midriff showing.

Why did I let Lola talk me into wearing it?

Black tights, thick black socks, and black Dr Marten's finish my look off.

I love my boots.

The kitten heels Lola tried getting me to wear were never going anywhere near my feet.

Touching up a smudge of thick black eye pencil from one of my eyes, the lashings of mascara I've put on isn't sending anyone weak at the knees and neither is my bright red-lipstick, or shoulder-length, backcombed, brown wavy hair. I suppose the red on the ends makes it a bit interesting but I'm nothing out of the ordinary, not like Lola.

Walking to the bar, the smell of cigarettes, alcohol, and piss cling to every surface, feeling my boots squelch underneath the filthy carpet much the same way my socks used to stick to my mother's bedroom carpet. If the old bitch could see me now? She'd be calling me every name under the sun.

Nothing she ever said was nice.

Not seeing her once in the last two years since I was flung out; I can't say the same for her filthy pervert friend, Kevin. He'd turned up at The Orchard unexpectedly one night, which had sent my anxiety into overdrive. It was one of the reasons I went looking for Lola. Kevin made the last six months at home a living hell for me.

I'll never forgive my mother for inviting him into the house.

Feeling my bumpy wrist, I'm suddenly panicking, terrified he will somehow find another way of walking back into my life when I least expect it.

I hate my mother even more for letting him hurt me like he did.

Eyeing every male in the club, staring, looking to see if any of them resemble the monster from my past, Greg the DJ's looking over at me, both thumbs in the air like he's read my mind.

The opening riff of ACDC's '*Highway to Hell*' starts playing and his raised thumbs wait for me to signal whether I like it or not. Chuckling, tapping my foot in time to the music with both my thumbs pointing up, I hope both monsters from my past are on their way, or as close to hell as they can get. But even I know that hell would be too good a place for them.

Blowing him a kiss, two young women in identical Madonna outfits next to me point at my clothes, laughing.

Bitches.

Killing them with my eyes, making my way to the bar, fiddling again with my crop-top as I wait in the queue, a cute barman I haven't seen before looks my way and smiles. Glancing around to see who the lucky woman might be he's smiling at, everyone seems busy, preoccupied with what they're doing.

Eyes locked with his, suddenly the floor beneath me turns to glue. I'm the only one in the room and there's a huge spotlight on me.

I can't move.

I can't move anything but my eyes, and now my neck is stuck, too, like I need to oil it.

Twisting away from his stare, the noise of the club booms back. It feels like I've been hypnotised and just come around.

Not looking his way for fear of freezing up again, I guess he had to be looking at someone behind me.

He wasn't looking at me like that. Who am I trying to kid?

Turning, watching the same people who all meet regularly on a Wednesday night, I recognise most of the same, sad, sorry faces who all wait to hook up with the paralytic chick/bloke at the end of the night. Using the seats at the back to fuck, touch up, or if they're lucky, get a blowjob, it's a place where people don't feel ashamed because everyone's pretty much doing the same thing.

Once, when I was waiting for Greg to pack up, I saw a woman so drunk her skirt was high up above her waist, legs wide open waiting for the men to frig her and her tits off. She didn't have a clue what was happening, but she sure as hell looked like she was enjoying it.

I later found out her name was Marian and that she had a right rough Irish husband at home who would've killed her if he'd found out.

She still regularly fucks around on him. She must have a death wish.

Following her blonde, wavy, backcombed eighties hair dancing on the floor, I'm amazed she has no shame in what she does. I think I've even seen her go upstairs with Ricki. Greg and Joni think she's a slut, but I'm sure they'd use her if they had no other choice. Huge smile, her pronounced large white teeth and big, round blue eyes lure men to her as 'Man Eater' plays in the background, sure Greg's put it on for her. In her early forties, tonight she looks great in her Olivia Newton John all-in-one, black leather jumpsuit which will soon be half way down her body, down the back, like every week.

Her bodily fluids and thousands of others before her will be on the covers back there, which is why I never go anywhere near it.

I'm afraid I might catch something.

It's a shame the place is so dingy. If Ricki gave as much attention to it as he does his outfits every week, it'd look half decent. The Rubik's Cube seats look so tatty and tired, once vibrant with colours that are now faded; the plastic is ripped in all sorts of places. People don't care if their drinks, spit or sweat spill all over them. Why should they? Ricki doesn't.

Just as *Kool & the Gang* tell us to celebrate, Greg changes the word celebrate to 'masturbate,' which the crowd loves. I've heard it that many times now I just laugh, wave, and give him a thumbs up.

The huge neon-yellow glasses he has on make him look like a grinning Cheshire cat, and his multi-coloured sequin jacket that's a tad too snug for his hefty six-foot-four frame, looks even funnier. Add to that his tight curly black hair waving wildly about as he bops around in his booth not keeping in time with the song, you'd swear he was wearing a wig, but it's his own hair, which makes it even better to watch.

Blowing me an imaginary kiss, I blow one back, dancing with both thumbs up, our secret move to let him know I like his choice of the next song. '*Bust a Move*' by *Young MC* is one of my favourites, tapping my foot in time to the beat with everyone else.

Greg loves his job, always trying to get people up to dance and request their favourite songs. I love his nerdy geeky way and the music he plays, often requesting more obscure songs I know he has. I remember the first night I met him and asked him to play '*Whip It*' by *Devo*. It had started us talking about music and that was pretty much it.

It's obvious he likes me more than a friend, but I've never thought of him romantically. To me he's like a brother, the same as Joni. Still, if I had to make a choice between the two, Joni would win hands down. Greg just isn't my type.

'Peek-a-Boo's' quirky intro by *Siouxie* is next on, but the crowd boos asking Greg to change it. Yelling at them, he waits until the first chorus of the song to change it. He knows how much I love Siouxie and I'm pretty sure he appreciates that I've sort of tried to look a little bit like her tonight. Both hands above his head in question, his sad face mouths sorry as he changes the song to *Split Enz's* 'I See Red.'

Giving him the thumbs up, he's suddenly not looking my way, instead staring at the new barman, eyes locked, like two Silverback gorillas ready to fight. Looking from each other to me, I look over my shoulder to see what or who they might be looking at.

I'm confused.

Ducking behind two tall men, spying on them through a slit in-between their bodies, just like that, the duel finishes and the barman prepares more drinks while Greg changes the lights from glitter to UV making all the dust on my clothes light up like little stars. The men I'm hiding behind give me a funny look, moving away, making me quickly hold onto the railings seeing little white floating dots smiling at each other on the dance floor. One woman's blotchy streaked face and clothes makes her look like someone's masturbated all over her; I'm desperately trying to figure out who she's come as. As if she's read my mind, she and her friend make their way to the bar, standing just in front of me as they queue. For once I wish Greg would shut up.

"Hey, girl, I had to get you off that dance floor, aye? All that UV light on your clothes and skin makes it look like someone has just wanked all over you. What the fuck? It looks bloody awful."

"Oh, come on. Can't you guess who I've come as? I thought you'd get it straight away, aye? No one's got it right yet."

As Greg starts playing the opening riffs to 'Come on Eileen,' asking the audience where she's gone, I suddenly get it.

"Aww, you dirty bitch. That's disgusting hee, hee, hee. It's come on Eileen, not cum on Eileen."

"A little cum on anyone never hurts. C'mon, we don't want to keep my adoring public waiting."

Nearly giving myself away laughing, they pass me, seeing the blotchy one up close. I've got to give it to her, it's bloody original and definitely asking for trouble. Laughing along with everyone around her, she obviously likes the attention as men grab their balls, moaning at her on her way back to the dancefloor full of floating white teeth. It's like a scene straight out of Alice in Wonderland.

Everyone, including Cum on Eileen's teeth and blotches, float in space, making sure to cover my mouth just in case the light somehow catches my teeth. The UV lights quickly change to lasers making people moan in protest as Greg points to Cum on Eileen who's laughing and bowing like the Queen, giving him permission to move on.

Red and green lines bounce off the crowd; one old man dancing with no rhythm whatsoever. I'd come here every week just to watch him and his hoary body gyrate in his skin-tight 70's jump-suit. He's trying to attract a group of young girls with his dance moves who are openly laughing and pointing at him, me included. It's turning into more like a comedy night rather than a club to dance. He might get lucky if he hangs around till the end. One of them might be drunk enough to let him feel them up, or if he's really lucky, Marian might give him a quick grope. I've seen it so many times before, I'm amazed any of those girls come back.

I'd die of embarrassment if it was me.

Boots sticking to the floor, moving toward the bar, it feels like I'm walking into a public toilet rather than across a club floor.

Successfully ordering my drinks from another barman, making my way through the crowd without managing to spill a drop, back at the table Lola isn't impressed.

"What bloody took you so long?"

Grabbing her drink, not even saying thank you, she stands, glaring at me, gulping it back in one.

I want to throw mine in her face and tell her to fuck off, but I do my usual.

"Whatever. It was really busy at the bar."

Glaring, handing me back the empty glass, she looks towards the dance floor.

"Wasn't too busy for you to stop and look around, was it, you dick. Why didn't you just buy two? This one's finished. Now you'll have to queue up at the bar again."

I hate it when she calls me names.

"I'll go get another one in a minute."

Brushing me aside, grabbing her glass back and scraping the last of the Baileys and ice through her straw, she throws it back at me while the men continue to encircle her, waiting for their chance.

I know the drill.

I'll be an invisible statue and watch the mating rituals until she's chosen whichever one she wants.

It's the same every week.

I don't know why men are so pathetic. They're such a sucker for a beautiful face.

Sensing someone's eyes on me, the new barman's staring at me again, smiling. Smiling back, head down, my face is on fire.

Why is he staring at me?

Why isn't he staring at Lola?

Everyone stares at her.

Sipping my drink, looking up, his eyes are on Lola.

Of course.

Exquisite, men lust her. Women, I'm sure, lust her, too. Tonight, her long, blonde, wavy hair is in a side pony-tail with a neon-orange head-band across her forehead. White liner on her inner lids, glittery purple eye-shadow on her eyelids, and electric-blue mascara lathered on her thick long lashes, makes her green eyes look even more perfect than usual.

She is an Amazonian 80's queen.

No wonder the barman can't keep his eyes off her.

Pouting and smiling at the ones she's singled out at having anywhere near a chance with her, I already feel sorry for them.

I don't think they care, though. All their eyes are glued to her boobs, practically falling out of her favourite, very low-cut, see-through, neon-yellow leotard. I'm sure her right breast is slightly bigger, but only I'd notice that.

Long toned legs in the sheerest tights, I hate to admit, is exactly how Olivia Newton-John should be done. I'm sure Olivia would've been a bit more modest with her cleavage, and perhaps she wouldn't have worn pink leg warmers or electric-blue kitten heels but, as electric-blue is a colour I love, I'll forgive her.

Standing on the gluey carpet, hand on hip, she is perfect, the complete package. It's obvious why she's the highest-earning girl at work, remembering the first time she'd walked into The Orchard.

I sat at my desk on a call and saw her out the window walking like she meant business. The door flew open, she marched in in the tiniest gold dress I'd ever seen and shouted.

"Where's your fucking madam? I'm going to make her a shit load of money."

Sharon had come out of her office to see what all the commotion was about, and the rest is history.

Watching Lola in action again tonight, that's all I ever seem to do. As if beauty wasn't enough? Closing my eyes, pleading to the Universe, I hope it hears me.

"Please don't let her see the new barman." Once she sees him, I'll have absolutely no chance.

Opening my eyes, the Universe doesn't give a rat's arse. Lola's staring straight over to him, confirming my worst nightmare. Bending down, just close enough for me to hear, she whispers in my ear.

"Do you like him, Jesse? He's a bit of a spunk, isn't he?"

Blowing him a kiss, waving at him like she already knows him, she turns back to her admirers resuming her pickings.

He's still watching her.

Fuck off Universe. Fuck off Lola.

What Lola wants Lola gets. I learned the hard way with Jim...

Chapter Four

'I can forgive you, but I will never trust you again.'

— Unknown

Five months earlier

Knock, knock.

Crap.

Squeezing out the last bit of wee, zipping up my jeans and running to answer the door, I don't see my undone shoelace, tumbling to the floor like a baby elephant.

Watching me through the glass, shading the sun with his hand, his worried face watches me pick myself up and brush myself off before opening the door.

Dark-brown curly hair the same shade as his concerned, deep-set eyes, flops over his clean-shaven face, where two cute deep dimples on each cheek wink at me.

Little stars escape from every part of my body, hardly hearing what he's saying.

"Are you alright? That was quite a tumble."

Gazing up into his rounded jaw, sparkling teeth smile nervously, noticing his two bottom teeth overlap, but that just adds to his cuteness.

Brushing the stars away, remembering what I'm doing. "Err I'm fine, better do up my shoelace before it happens again."

Bending, checking out his tight black jeans clinging to long muscly legs, he wears a Pink Floyd t-shirt which hangs from his short lean torso.

He likes his music.

Tick.

A retro looking red and white bomber jacket wrapped tightly around his broad shoulders looks cool, as does his black lace-up trainers, no socks, which have a tiny fleck of what looks like mud on the top of them.

His build is exactly my type and add to that his dimples and dark eyes, I'm ready planning our wedding.

Catching a whiff of his cologne, mmm, all I can smell is the ocean.

I didn't know what to expect when Celeste, my favourite of The Orchard girls, asked me to help her out. I certainly wasn't expecting anything like the spunk standing in front of me now.

"I'm here about the room? I'm Jim"

Extending his hand to mine, I go to shake it, shocked at the crack of electricity that suddenly passes between us. Answering his chest, rubbing my hand on my jeans, I can't look at him.

"I'm Jesse, Celeste is stuck covering a shift at work so has asked me to show you around. Hope you don't mind?"

Celeste is the last person I'd ever have expected to see in a place like The Orchard. Very calm, always doing yoga in between clients, I love her and her holistic ways. Feng shui-Ing her room upstairs at work to encourage as much 'positive' energy as she can whilst 'entertaining' her clients, makes me love her more.

"Feeling the experience is better for the soul."

Believing every word she says, the proof is in the pudding as all her clients book her weeks in advance, stating they feel cleansed and energised after an hour with her.

Not once in the two years I've worked at The Orchard has any client of hers complained about being cleansed whilst having their balls emptied.

Only Celeste could pull *that* one off.

Scented candles used to cleanse men's auras diffuse around The Orchard making not only her room, but every room, smell lovely and clean. Crystals of all colours adorn every available space, ensuring to lap up any energy she feels could affect the ambience.

"I feel their energy as soon as they walk in. Can't have any of that negative shit spoiling the experience for us girls now, can we."

Since Lola has started the crystals have increased, even extending to the lift.

A dinky five-foot four-inches tall, Celeste's perfect hourglass figure makes her a firm favourite with the men. Add to that her luxurious long, ash-blonde, wavy hair, green eyes, high cheekbones, and full lips, she is exotic and beautiful. The tiniest of bumps in the middle of her nose and a miniscule mole above her lips only adds to her charm. Her oval face looks especially beautiful in the black round glasses she wears for reading, men often asking her to leave them on.

Level-headed, calm, soft-spoken and one of the only girls not doing drugs, she is one of the few people at work I've connected with, and today she has been caught covering another girl's shift so has asked me to go meet her potential new flatmate.

"The stars are aligned, Jesse. Today you're going to meet someone special, I can feel something wonderful is about to happen."

Sharon had not been happy about covering the phones, but just this once had let me help out.

"You hurry back, ok? I don't like to answer phone. Too hard when men want 'special' things. You work an extra hour tomorrow, ok?"

I could've kicked myself a million times for not taking a cab. Instead, I'd jumped on the bus and spent the whole time standing under the smelliest man alive, and if that hadn't been bad enough, some stupid teenage boy had opened a window while we were travelling through the tunnel and let in all the smelly car exhaust fumes which had made my throat feel like it'd been scratched the shit out of with a hundred nails. I'd thought I was going to pass out. The smelly man, I swear, stunk of glue, beer, and onions; the combination so nauseating, I'd nearly vomited all over his filthy bare feet. Thankfully I'd gotten off at the stop straight after the tunnel.

I don't know why, but I felt sorry for him and had snuck ten dollars into his baggy trackpants pocket as I'd got off. He'd waved at me with a floppy hand and vacant eyes and the poor woman who'd taken my place underneath him had already had her hand up to her nose before the doors had closed. Her eyes were almost as sad as Kermit the frogs on the filthy man's vest.

Crossing the road, Celeste's little two-bedroom house is right at the end of the street next to a zig-zag path up to the woods. Thankfully it had only taken about two-minutes to walk from the bus stop.

Telling me he works in the music industry (tick), Jim and I instantly click over what music each other likes, pointing to his *Pink Floyd* t-shirt, asking what his favourite song of theirs is.

Stars floating around my head again, his dimples take centre stage.

"Got to be '*Wish You Were Here*.' The whole album is good if you ask me."

Smiling and agreeing, he tells me he's a member of an indie band and plays lead guitar, (tick).

Is this a set-up by Celeste?

I've never felt this much connection with anyone.

Ever.

Arriving at the kitchen, his six-foot-five-inch frame is a whole foot taller than mine, ducking to get through the door. Standing in the middle of the room, he seems out of place, looking around, eyes focusing on the tiny round table he's standing beside. Tatty with bits of blue paint and burn marks from cigarettes, there seems to be a pattern etched into the wood. Curious to see what it is, both our heads bend to take in the markings.

My heart flips.

A massive cock smiles up at us and I don't mean the chicken kind.

Eyes wide, awkwardly smiling at each other, we look anywhere but the table.

"I think Celeste needs to buy a tablecloth. Unless you want to add to the very excellent artwork?"

Laughing, looking back at the thick cock exploding with liquid out the top of its knob, whoever drew it had no imagination.

Quickly covering it with a plate I've seen in the sink, my heart does a second flip gazing towards the cupboards. Embarrassed, the pale-blue of the wood is hardly seen through the stickers covering them.

Wishing I'd remembered, it'd been a while since I'd visited, the cock was definitely not here last time, but the stickers?

I knew about them.

The Universe hates me.

Concentrating on a particularly busty, dark-haired girl with long wavy hair, she wears nothing but a lacy black G-string and thigh-high boots, squatting, legs spread wide. Breasts winking straight at Jim, he looks from the sticker to me, smiling nervously, reaching into his coat pocket to retrieve his small, rounded frames. Walking up to the cupboards for a better look, his nose is inches from her breasts.

"They're really something."

Questioning eyes look from the woman's cleavage to mine, quickly covering my own with my cardigan, pointing to the scented candles on each window sill, hoping to steer the conversation, and his eyes, elsewhere.

"Mmm the lavender smells divine don't you think? It's my favourite scent by far."

Smiling, nodding, he spots the tapestry draped over the entire main kitchen wall.

Colourful life trees resplendent with blue branches cover the entire space with orange, red, yellow, and green leaves.

"Very different, isn't it?"

Unsure whether he's talking to himself or me, he stands, arms folded over each other gazing at the scene.

"I think it's fabulous."

Turning the lights on for better effect, fairy lights attached very carefully to the tops of the cupboards make it look like an ethereal playground.

Even the stickers fit in, in a weird fantastical way.

The little blue fridge freezer in the corner hums loudly as we inspect the rest of the kitchen. Next to a tiny gas oven and hob, I unlock the light-blue back door and walk out to a minuscule patio area where Celeste has clothes hanging, drying in the sun. As luck wouldn't have it, a line of tiny G-strings of all different colours gently sway in the breeze.

"She loves her colours. Shall we move on to the bedroom?"

I'm so nervous around him.

Smirking, dimples on show again, I actually think he's enjoying my discomfort.

A few steps down the narrow hallway we're in a spacious double bedroom decorated with yet another tapestry. This one is of a forest of sunlight, transforming the bedroom into a private paradise.

The big double bed looks directly into woodland as the beaming sun makes its way through their branches. Patches of light on the woodland floor make it look rather magnificent. Transfixed, we gaze, smiling at it.

"That's really something," he beams.

His dimples agree.

The window sill, sprayed with succulents of all different sizes, also houses scented pine candles making us imagine we are actually in the woods. More candles sit on top of some very sad looking

wooden drawers directly underneath the window. A runner decorated with ivy sits across the top of them adding to the ambience. To
the right of the tapestry, an old oak wardrobe proudly looks on,
making the aesthetic of the room cohesive; under the bed a thick dark
green carpet simulates the woodland floor. At each side of the bed sits
a table recycled from old tree stumps and above, in the centre of the
ceiling, hangs a lampshade spectacularly crafted from metal, the trees
and branches stretching around so when lit, the light escapes through
each gap casting the woods against the ceiling and walls.

The room really does look enchanted.

Celeste has done wonders.

If I didn't already live at The Orchard, I'd move here in a
heartbeat.

"This really is something," he says, not taking his eyes off the
tapestry.

"Shall we move to the lounge?"

The next room, in comparison, is quite tame with only a couple
of two-seater brown leather lounge sofas, a coffee table made out of
the same tree stump as the bedroom tables, and a tiny television.

"Obviously Celeste doesn't spend too much time in here."

No tapestry, there's only a few pictures of some generic flowers
on the walls which seems rather dull.

"No tapestry in here then?" he says, walking to the big bay
window pointing to the zig-zag path up to the woods. Asking where it
leads, I tell him Celeste likes to do her yoga in the outdoor space.

"You'll love it up there, loads of space to play your guitar in the
fresh air."

Asking to look at the kitchen again to see what things he might
need to bring; his eyes once again focus on the sticker of the busty
squatting model, looking from me to her, eyes questioning if it's me.

Celeste's zen is wasted on him.

Blushing, looking away, embarrassed, I'm sure he's enjoying it.

"Great. Thanks. I'll defo take it. The tapestries have won me over
and as it's quite close to where I work it'll be perfect."

"Wow, that was quick. I thought you were in a band. Is that not your work?"

"No, I'm a Photographic Lab Technician by day. It's just through the tunnel, about a twenty-minute walk."

"Cool, I'll let Celeste know you want it."

Taking his number and telling him Celeste will get back to him after she checks his references, I walk him to the door and shake his hand.

Crack.

Jumping in shock - again - we both rub our hands on our jeans, smiling nervously. His dimples start to speak.

"Hope I see you around, Jesse."

Bouncing the few steps to the gate in a couple of strides, he and his dimples look back, wave, and walk towards the end of the street, meanwhile the butterflies in my stomach join the stars as they escape from every space.

I'm so in love.

Hurrying back to work, this time taking a cab, Sharon's happy to see me relieving her from phone duties.

Reporting back to Celeste a little later that Jim wants the room; "He especially likes your busty women stickers. I bloody forgot they were there."

"Sorry hunny, I haven't got round to covering them up yet. I don't even know if I want to. I quite like them in an odd way. Female solidarity."

Pumping the air like a warrior, I sort of agree with her.

"They're actually quite beautiful, Jesse. One of them looks so much like you."

"Yeah, I thought that too when he kept looking from her boobs to mine and then back again."

Laughing, I add the torture of the unfortunate cigarette mark on the table.

"It looks like a cock! We both just stood there awkwardly looking at it. When did you do that? It wasn't there the last time I visited?"

"Oh God, I'm so sorry, Jesse. I meant to bloody cover it up. One of my ex-boyfriends had an idea one night to do it when he was whacked off his face on mushrooms. I'll make sure to get a cover for it tomorrow. Thank you so much for doing this for me. I owe you big time."

"You bloody do. I'll tell you about the bus ride later on. My days are usually quite boring. This will be right up there as one to remember. By the way, you've decorated the place beautifully. The tapestries, the light shade in the bedroom, the plants, everything. Please, help me with my space? You're so good at it all. I'd really appreciate your help. I'll buy you a tablecloth as thanks."

"Sure thing. Any time. Just let me know when you need me and maybe one day when we're both free we can have a look? Anyway, enough of that. Tell me, what was he like?"

Gushing, I tell Celeste everything, not forgetting to include Jim's to die for dimples and that he's in a band. Little stars floating around my head, it's obvious I like him.

"Mmm, not obvious you fancy him, Jesse. Go for it. He sounds gorgeous. I'm a bit miffed I didn't go, now!"

"What? I can't. He won't like me. I'm nowhere near pretty enough, and I'm the wrong shape."

"You're gorgeous. All you got to do is channel it. He'd be a dick to turn you down."

"Easy for you, you've got loads of men eating out of your hands. Jim will never want me."

"Who are you kidding? Of course, he will. I have his number. Ring him. What's the worst that could happen?"

Telling all the girls that I like him, Celeste comes clean telling me they all know and agree, including Sharon, that I should ask him out once he's moved in.

That's the last thing I need, to be rejected.

No. I will definitely not be making a fool of myself. I know they're all just trying to help and want to see me happy but, it's something I just can't do. There is no way I will be asking anyone out.

Ever.

I wish Gail was still around. She would've helped. She would've known what to do.

A week later, sitting with the girls in the back in-between clients, Celeste is still hassling me to ring Jim. I want to, but I'm a wuss, terrified he'll say no and I'll make a first-class fool of myself.

But those dimples. They've even come to me in my dreams.

All I've sung for days is 'I *Think I Love You*' by the *Voice of the Beehive*, envisioning walking up the aisle to it. I'm pathetic!

"Ring him. You've got nothing to lose."

"I can't do that."

Those dimples, though.

"Ha! Get a life. You won't have the guts."

Lola sneers behind me as the other girls rush to my defence.

Ramona, the new girl, politely suggests.

"Just be yourself, Jesse. A lot of my friends say that men actually like it better when you act normal. I don't know because they take one look at me and don't give a shit what's on the inside. Don't take this the wrong way, but, you're lucky you're only average looking. At least men will give you a chance and not want you as a trophy on the end of their arms. I'd love to know how that feels. That's why I like women, too. They're not as fussy. Tell you what, if he doesn't have you, I will. You're just my type."

Winking, blowing me a kiss, I'm a little confused at the back-handed compliment. She's definitely coming onto me and I'm not sure whether I'm completely comfortable with it. Lola definitely isn't; growling, sneering at her.

"I don't know what you're talking about. Who said you were pretty?"

Sharon walks in to see what we're doing raising her eyes at Ramona and Lola.

"Now, now girls, you be nice. You two are my best girls. You must be friends."

The conversations I've had with Sharon. She's told me Lola and Ramona have the potential to make her rich beyond her wildest dreams, but knows that won't happen if she doesn't find a way of making them get along.

"Having them both on my books is a double gift and I want to keep them right where the dollar signs are."

Ramona has made more in her first two weeks than Lola has made in four months and that's only with male clients. When women start to come, Ramona will be Queen of The Orchard and that is something Lola won't be able to bear.

Everybody knows it.

Sharon knows it, too.

Her dream of the two girls working together as a double act fading before her eyes, right now she has to keep them apart before they kill each other. She said landing Ramona had been one of her biggest coups.

Watching as she takes Ramona and Lola by the hand, they both flinch away from each other.

"If only you girls could get along. My mother wouldn't have put up with you fighting. No matter how gorgeous you were, if you did not get along with another girl, you were out! You lucky I'm not like her. I wish you had met her. You would have loved her."

"What was she like, Sharon? Tell us, please? You've never really opened up about your life growing up. Tell us about your mother and what it was like back then. It'll at least shut Lola and Ramona up for a second."

Raising their hands to complain, Sharon's hand tells them to stop, both huffing, crossing their hands over their chests. Waiting for silence, Sharon begins to tell us her story.

Chapter Five
Sharon

"When I first came to New Zealand as a little girl I thought my life would end. My mother fell in love and married Thomas, a man I did not like at all. I'm sure he did not like me, too, and just wanted my mother and wished me gone.

I was living in Australia at the time and cried and cried when we had to leave. It was a place I loved and the people we lived with were very good to me. They looked after me and loved me. When my mother met Thomas, my life changed."

"How did it change, Sharon?"

"Wait, Jesse. You must be patient. I will tell all."

"Ok, sorry. I'll shut up."

"Never mind. Now, I will start from the beginning. I was born Qiang Yang on September 11th 1941 in Sham Shui Po, a slum in Hong Kong. Qiang means 'strong' in Chinese. My mother chose it because she wanted me to be strong and powerful, like the sun, which is the meaning of Yang. She always told me I was her strong sunshine."

"I love that. Strong sunshine. Your mother was right, Sharon."

"Yes, I think she was, Celeste. I got my strength from my mother.

Her name was Ai. She was one of 10,000 women raped when Japan took over. She said it was the worst time of her life. My father was a Japanese soldier who raped her. She was only fifteen."

"Omg. That's awful, Sharon. Your poor mother."

"She told me it was very awful, Lola. Back then, Japanese soldiers didn't care how old you were. I only remember a little from my childhood in Hong Kong. My mother told me a lot. She told me she watched people burn, even her own mother and father, but first the soldiers made her watch them rape her mother, sister and other women and children. Then she watched them be killed."

"Oh God. I don't know if I want to hear anymore. I'm already crying."

"It gets worse, Jesse. But, it important for all you girls to hear what went on back then. It might make you hate each other less. My mother said she was one of the lucky ones who escaped and that the Japanese soldiers even went to hospitals to kill English soldiers who were injured. They killed nurses and doctors who were looking after them, too."

"Why are people so evil to each other? Why can't we all just live in peace and love each other?"

"That is what I want you and Lola to do, Ramona."

Raising her eyebrows at me, Ramona hunches her shoulders and smiles. I think she understands what I mean. Lola's not backing down, though, and kills Ramona with her eyes.

"Unfortunately, the world is not like that. War has been going on long time. I doubt it will ever end. My mother told me the Japanese cut off the English soldiers' noses, arms, legs, ears, and eyes with swords and then raped the nurses on top of soldiers' bodies."

"Please tell me that isn't true, Sharon?"

"It is true, Jesse, because I read it later when I was older. My mother also told me one nurse nearly had her head completely cut off."

"I hate people so much. I hate war. Your poor mother."

"Yes, I felt the same. I never thought people could be so cruel. My mother was in hospital having me when it happened to the nurse. The soldiers saw my mother and lined up to rape her while I was still in her belly, so she ran when they finished and said she needed the toilet and escaped out a window before they had time to kill her, kill me."

Gasping, all the girls faces are sad listening to my story. Jesse, Celeste and Ramona are crying. Lola is just staring ahead, like she's frozen.

"I was born in a house in a slum. My mother's friend, Li, helped. Thank God it was not too difficult for my mother to give birth otherwise I might have died. Li helped and I was born healthy. I don't know how my mother survived."

"I know if it was me, I wouldn't have lived more than five minutes."

"You don't know what you would do, Jesse. You have to be in situation to know. My mother said it was very hard because she was so young when she had me, but I always felt her love. She never punished me for being born which I love her more for. She told me it was not my fault the soldier hurt her, that I was a blessing, her strong sun, even though at times she thought she might not want me. I don't know if I would have kept my baby after being raped. Especially if I was only fifteen and a virgin."

"Your mother was so strong, Sharon. I've never heard anything like this ever before. I wish I could've met her."

"My mother was strong. You would have loved her, Jesse. She would've loved you, too."

"What did she do?"

"She escaped to the forest to look after me, but she had to look out for Japanese soldiers who wanted to kill us. She said it came really close one time, and that she knew it was time to get out of Hong Kong for good. It was too much terror for her."

"Where did she go?"

"One day, she waited by the docks to escape on a boat to Australia. It was the exact day I turned four. Japan had already surrendered so I don't know why she went. I remember there being so much joy when she heard the news. She took me down to docks and told me to be quiet and to follow her onto a ship. We hid in a box and watched lots of other women and children who were also leaving Hong Kong. They were white women and children, not like me and Mother. I remember asking my mother why we were hiding?"

"What did she say?"

"She just said to be quiet. The boat ride made me very sick. The sea was very angry and I could not eat for two days and nights. When we arrived in the Philippines, we looked out of the box and could not believe how dead the harbour looked. Of course, back then I did not know it was Philippines. The only place I knew was Hong Kong. There were so many ships bombed, it looked like a ship graveyard. Some ships we could not see because they had already sunk into the water and only had a mast left. We were looking so hard that we did not see a woman watching us. Her name was Muriel and her daughter was Katy. They tried to talk but we could not understand. We thought they wanted to take us to the Japanese soldiers so my mother panicked and screamed. It took a long time for Muriel to get us out, but when she did, she took us to a place where we could rest and gave us food."

"Thank God! I bet you were so relieved?"

"Yes, we were, Lola, but we could not speak English. Muriel was so kind. A lovely lady. Her daughter and I played even though we could not speak to each other. I know she liked me because she smiled and always took my hand. It was such a happy time after all the unhappiness of Hong Kong. We rested then had to go back to another ship two days later and sail to Singapore. I did not want to get back on the boat, but this time the water was more calm, not so angry. I was happier because my stomach behaved."

"What happened in Singapore?"

"In Singapore we had to change to another boat again and when we left we met a very pretty lady named Lady Mountbatten who went on another boat to England. I did not know what England was back then. Now of course I do. She was with her husband who looked very smart. I shook his hand but I do not know what he said to me. I wish I could remember. We walked onto other boat named Tamaroa and then sailed to Australia. Other children had a party with me, and I played with them and made new friends. My mother did not make friends because she could not speak English. There was lots of confusion why we were even on the boat, but they let us stay."

"Why do you think they let you stay, Sharon? You were so lucky."

"Yes, we were very lucky, Jesse. I think they let us stay because they felt sorry for us. On 16th October 1945 we arrived in Melbourne at Princess Pier. I remember there was lots of music. People waved flags and had so much joy and happiness. I kept looking around not believing my eyes."

"Yay! You made it. Where did you stay?"

"Yes, we did make it finally to Australia, Ramona, but we did not have passports, so the lovely lady Muriel explained to a gentleman she was helping us to get one and the gentleman let us go with her and she helped us with new paperwork. Australia was beautiful, huge, full of trees and very green. We were allowed to stay with Muriel and Katy at her Aunty Mavis's house for a long time. Aunty Mavis taught us English and showed us how to cook and use the oven. My mother even tried to show them how to make Chinese food, but they did not like it. I learned how to dry dishes. One time I nearly dropped a beautiful plate, so after that I was not allowed to dry dishes anymore. My mother and I slowly learned English and two years later moved out of Auntie's house because my mother met a man named Thomas. He was a sailor from New Zealand, across the water. He had to work many hours. She loved him and married him but I do not think Aunty liked him. She did not smile at the wedding and neither did Muriel or Katy. They explained to my mother he was no good, but she did not listen to them and let him take us to Wellington. I did not want to go and begged my mother to stay in Australia with Muriel and Katy but she would not listen to me. I had to go."

"Oh, wow! So that's how you came to New Zealand? I never knew that, Sharon."

"I haven't told many people, Jesse. It was not a happy time for me. Everyone cried at the harbour when we left. I was so sad to never see Katy again. She gave me a beautiful, jewelled egg to take. I still have it. I think it is called Faberge. I'm not sure."

"I've seen it in your office. It's beautiful."

"Never touch my egg, please. It is very precious to me. I will leave it to you, Jesse, when I die because you are Gail's niece and like a daughter to me."

"Don't make me cry, Sharon. I'll treasure it forever, but it'll be a long time before that happens. Go on with your story. What happened in Wellington?"

"In Wellington Thomas started to beat my mother. I remember lots of shouting and crying. Thomas tried to touch me one night, so my mother took me to live on the streets for a long time until she found another place to live. I was so sad. It was a very dangerous time. Some men would want me and not my mother who, they said, was too old. She was very worried. One day she took me to a place called The Orchard. The owner was very nice and let us live there, but Mother had to work upstairs a lot and I had to stay in a room, at the back, on my own."

"Omg, that's how you came to live in The Orchard. Who would've known?"

"Yes, I stayed in the house and eventually started school during the day and learned more English. My mother changed my name to Sharon so I would be more accepted. My new friends told me I lived in a naughty house. I did not know what they meant 'naughty house' but when I grew up I knew what they meant. I begged my mother to leave, but she would not, saying the owner, an old lady name Stella, loved us like we were her own children, so we stayed. After Stella died she left everything, including the house, to my mother. I could not believe she gave us everything, just like that!"

"Wow! You don't know how lucky you were, Sharon. Tons of people would have given both their legs to get a place like this."

"Yes, I know how lucky we were. I thank God every day for making us meet Stella. When she died, Thomas heard and came to try to take half of the house, but Mother had a new boyfriend by then who said he would hurt Thomas if he did not go away, so he never came back."

"Thank God!"

"Yes, God work in mysterious ways. I lived at The Orchard and watched how my mother ran the place. When her new boyfriend left her she told me every night at bedtime to never meet a man because he would take everything off me, so I did not."

"Your mother had the right idea, Sharon. Men are shits!"

"Not all men are shits, Lola. Some are very good. My poor mother died suddenly of a heart attack when I was only eighteen. It was the saddest day of my life. She left everything to me and I had to take over her job at The Orchard, which was very hard. Some women did not want me for their boss because I was so young, so they left. Most of the other women stayed."

"How sad, Sharon. You lost your mother so young."

"Yes, I was sad for a very long time. It wasn't until seventeen years later that my life began to get better."

"How?"

"One day a young girl started to come and wait outside for food. Every Sunday she came. I think she must have only been young, maybe sixteen or seventeen. She did not talk to me straight away and it took a long time for her to speak to me."

"I know who this is! You're talking about my aunt Gail, aren't you."

"Yes, Jesse. One Sunday, I saw Gail's belly had grown. I watched it grow and grow and thought I would see the baby when it came, but she did not come back for four weeks. The next time I saw her the baby inside her belly was gone and all she did was cry. I did not see her for six months after that and then suddenly she came back and asked to work for me. I did not ask what happened to her baby. She looked so sad."

"It killed her to lose her babies. Just the brief time I spent with her was enough for me to understand how much that affected her. I would have loved her to have found them."

"We all would've loved that, Jesse. When I met Gail she told me she had been on the streets a long time so could bring girls to work. I gave her money and helped her make her own house on the streets. She eventually told me about her sister who she loved very much and could never see again because of her evil mother. I was so sad for Gail. She helped me very much back then even though she was sad, too. I asked her to come live at The Orchard with me, but she did not want to and said too many people needed her on the streets. We were best friends, even though she was so much younger than me, and then Gigi, too, when she started to clean for me. She was from Portugal but had lived a long time in New Zealand. I loved them both like they were my little sisters."

"I saw the place you helped Gail build. It was awesome! I love Gigi, too. She's a crack up. She never stops telling Lola how much she reminds her of Gail."

"Yes, she tells me that, too, Jesse."

Looking across to Lola, she doesn't look happy. I know she wants to say something, but her lips are glued shut. Nodding to her, she nods quickly back and gives me a little smile to let me know she's not mad at me. She's a good girl. I wish she would show everyone else she is.

"Gail asked to send me a girl who reminded her of her sister. I did not want her because I could see she was too young for business, so I gave her a job on reception."

Turning to Jesse and smiling, she's smiling back.

"It was such a shock for me to find out you were Gail's long-lost niece, Jesse. I remember how my heart broke into a million tiny

49

pieces because I knew how much Gail had wanted to find her sister. I think finding you broke her heart. I was so sad she never met the sister she loved so much, again."

"Believe me Sharon, she would not have wanted to see my mother again."

"I know, Jesse. That's why I promised I would look after you like my own family. I did that for Gail. I'm so happy you and beautiful Samantha live here now. It makes me feel like I still have a little bit of Gail with me. Without you, The Orchard would not look so modern, so beautiful. Now I have a lot more clients because of it. I also have Ramona who has taken on more clients. I think you girls would have a lot more work to do if she were not here."

Looking over at Lola, she doesn't like Ramona being here at The Orchard. It threatens her top spot. Lola makes a lot more money than the other girls and is not very nice to them. I am fed up with her fighting with them. Two weeks ago, when Ramona started work here, Lola became very angry. I couldn't pass the opportunity up. Girls like Ramona do not come around the corner too often...

...Out at my favourite Turkish restaurant Hazar in Wellington; I've arranged to meet my friends here because the food is so good. I also like the owner, Abdul, who I have known for a very long time. Coming to greet me with a kiss on my cheek, he always asks how business is going.

"It good, going ok. I have girl who is very beautiful, all the men love her. You come. I give you her for free."

"Ha! You know my wife would kill me. Keep an eye out for the dancer tonight. She could be your next big thing. You can have her for a good price."

I shoo, shoo him off.

"You go away you naughty boy. You are always saying that."

Slapping me on the shoulder, tapping his nose and putting two front fingers from his eyes to the curtain for me to watch, suddenly the lights dim and slow sexy music begins to play.

Behind a red velvet curtain something starts to move. Slowly one pale leg moves like a snake that wants to hypnotise me. More of her body comes, her pink tassels on her smooth silky pink skirt has lots of beautiful shiny jewels on it. Her hip, half her tiny stomach and an arm move in time to the music and bit by bit her whole body comes and still her back is to the audience. Long black hair brushes over her top, turning around with her head still down swaying to the music, and suddenly the lights turn off and everyone jumps. Lights back on, I see her face and think she is not real.

Abdul was right.

Her thick, long, black hair moves back and forth to the music and her big green eyes with long curly eyelashes don't want me to stop looking.

Moving her hips in perfect time to the music, her flat belly with a diamond inside lifts and drops, twists, rolls, making my eyes look to her small, perfect, round breasts which are pushed up by the help of a pink tassel bra, which also has beautiful jewels on it.

She has everyone under her spell.

Smooth pale skin moves like I have never seen before, her whole body vibrates and shimmies to slow Turkish music. Both men and women hold out so much money desperate to touch her, be near her. Sliding over to take their money, she lets them touch her when they pin money to the side of her costume and underneath her bra strap.

I want her so much to come work for me.

She comes to me and I give her lots of money, looking straight in her eyes, smiling.

The rest is history.

Offering her double what she makes belly dancing, I pay Abdul a hefty price and Ramona comes to join The Orchard crew.

"Not just a pretty face eh? Ha, ha."

... The girls' reaction was mixed. Most of them were fine and welcomed Ramona, but I saw a few who looked at her with very green eyes. They were worried they would not earn as much money once the men saw Ramona, and said it was bad enough having to compete with Lola let alone another beautiful girl. Lola disliked Ramona from the start and sparks have flown. I don't know why, but I have a funny feeling that the sparks are not because they do not like each other.

I've been in the business for a long time now and know Ramona will ruffle a few feathers, but they will learn to accept her as family, just like they did Lola.

The money I will make having Ramona on the books is too good an opportunity to pass up and now she tells me she like girls too, finally, after years of wanting to open up a special room for women, I will be able to offer services to them.

Most of the girls are very good about Ramona's bisexuality and think it is great she knows what she wants and is not afraid to show it. But I've noticed how much Ramona likes Jesse and worry the sparks are going to fly with Lola again.

"Bet you're kicking yourself for signing Ramona up now, aren't you, Sharon?"

"Shut up, Lola! Don't bring the mood down. Sharon's just opened up about her life and you want to put a downer on the conversation. Just live with the fact that I'm here to stay, you bitch! Jesse's happy to have me here, aren't you?"

The air, thick with tension could be cut with a knife. Jesse, by the looks of it doesn't want to get stuck in the middle with Ramona and Lola.

"I didn't think Jesse was your type. Hands off, bitch. Stay away from her. She's my friend, not yours. Don't think she'll ever be interested in you. She likes men and dicks. You will never be anything she wants."

"Threatened, are we? Not everyone does as they're told by you, Lola."

Ramona speaks with a voice so calm; she is clearly not scared of Lola. I am afraid of what might happen.

Before anyone knows, Lola's up and pointing her finger right into Ramona's face.

"Threatened by what? You? Please! I've been around girls like you my whole life. Just keep to the ones you can flutter your pretty little eyelashes at, you manipulative bitch. There are some of us who can see right through you."

Why do these two beautiful girls hate each other so much?

From what Jesse's told me, Ramona thinks Lola uses her beauty the wrong way and Lola thinks Ramona is full of herself, needs bringing down a peg or two.

"I'll show you who's boss around here, Crapmona."

"Yeah? You'll be eating out of my hands, and a few other places I want soon enough."

Staring at each other, Lola jumps to grab Ramona, but thankfully the other girls stop her.

"You fucking bitch. I won't be eating anywhere near you or your ugly muff."

"Jealous, are you? You're not my type, anyway. Sorry, I prefer them a little more 'petite' than you."

Celeste tries to break them up. I can see the chemistry between the two girls isn't all bad and think maybe this will work in my favour after all.

"Sorry Sharon, I'll get these two out of your hair in a minute. Before your story, we were trying to persuade Jesse to ring up Jim, remember the boy I said she liked? We said she should ask him out. What do you think? A good idea?"

"Yes. Jesse, you need to find boyfriend, stop the girls fighting over you!"

"Very funny, Sharon. For your information, I like dick."

Pushing Lola away from Ramona, Celeste picks up the phone and dials Jim's number before Jesse can say no. Phone on loud speaker, we all hear Jim's voice.

"Hello Jim speaking."

Everyone freezes. Jesse panics, looking at Celeste who's telling her to speak with her hands.

Lola and Ramona just glare at each other.

"Err hi, Jim... it's Jesse. I showed you around my friend Celeste's flat just over a week ago?"

"Oh yeah, I remember, how are you?"

"Um, I'm good, thanks. I was, um, just wondering, um, whether you'd maybe like to, um, meet up for a drink one night?"

Jesse's hand is on her heart and now her face looks like she wants to be sick.

"Yeah sure, Jesse, that sounds great. How about tonight? I'm free."

"No it's Thursday, I had my day off yesterday."

"I've got a gig this Saturday, how about you come along to that and we can grab a drink after?"

"I work on Saturday too, sorry. How about next Wednesday? It's my night off."

"No worries, sure. Sounds good. I'll come pick you up at yours."

"No! I'll meet you in town. Do you know Holics Express? It's a cool little cocktail bar down past Courtney Place."

"Yeah, I know it. Good choice. Cool, ok. See you at about seven?"

"Great, look forward to it. Bye."

Hanging up the phone, Jesse looks so pale and ill I think she's going to pass out.

"Omg, he said yes."

Hugging Jesse, Celeste squeals and Lola sneers, not happy. Ramona looks very happy for Jesse and kisses her on the cheek.

"Well done. Told you he'd be crazy to say no. I'll be here if you ever need it."

Blowing Lola a kiss before she walks off, Lola's look could kill her. "Whatever bitch."

This is not good.

"Now, now girls, you be nice. Lola. She is a nice girl. You give Ramona a chance, ok? Promise? I need you two to be friends. Now go give Jesse a hug and then all of you get back to work. I need to go lie down. You girls make me so tired."

Chapter Six
Jesse

Still looking at the phone, I think I might faint.

Did I really just ask Jim out?

Vomiting into the rubbish bin, I feel stupid.

"What have I just done? I'm a fool. Lola, do you think the Universe is finally trying to help me out?"

"Ha. You'll spew again because you can't handle it, you wuss. He only said yes because he felt sorry for you. Nah, only joking. Where did he say his gig was on Saturday?"

Uncomfortable why she's asking, I'm too busy to worry about it. It's too late anyway, Sharon's just yelled from the back to get back to work.

Six torturous days later, my nerves are overtaking my whole body as everyone at The Orchard, even Sharon, wishes me luck for my date.

"Just be yourself. He will love you just the way you are," Ramona reassures me.

I'm not even sure I like myself at the moment.

Doubting whether there really was a spark between us, was Lola right? Did he only say yes out of pity? There'd definitely been flirting, chemistry, or had I imagined it because I'd wanted more than anything to believe that someone might be interested in me other than Greg the DJ or Ramona.

It's too late, I can't pull out now.

Mind completely blank, I can't decide what to wear, staring at the clothes sprawled out all over my bed with dread.

I'm so nervous for my first ever date.

I know who'll tell me the truth. Celeste will help and as luck has it, it's her day off, ringing to see if I can pop around, sure the nervousness in my voice shows.

"Sure, hunny, how exciting. Come for a couple of drinks to help calm your nerves and I'll cleanse your aura, too. It will make you more open, less stressed. That and a few drinks will have him eating out of your hands. I'll run you a bubble bath, put on a few candles for you and help you with your hair and makeup. It'll be fab. Bring all your clothes so we can go through the outfits one by one. I'll bring the ones you don't use when I come back to work tomorrow. I'm popping out to get a few things so if I'm not here when you arrive you know where the spare key is. Let yourself in. I won't be far behind. Jim's been at his friend's the last couple of nights so don't worry, you won't see him before your date."

Catching a cab to hers, humming a song all the way, something feels uneasy.

I don't know why.

Paying the cab, jumping out and hauling my huge bags up the three stairs to the house, I knock, waiting to see if Celeste is there. No-one answers, quickly checking to see if anyone is watching before retrieving the key from under the laughing Buddha statue on the front porch and letting myself in, shouting to see if she's out the back. Hearing noises, wondering if she has company, I shout.

"Celeste, it's me. Celeste, it's me, where are you?"

Click.

The door to Jim's room opens.

The floor beneath my feet caves in.

Frozen, holding my breath, I don't want to see what's in front of me, dropping my bags to the carpet.

Lola smirks, turns, and passionately kisses Jim, making sure to shove as much tongue down his throat as she can.

He hasn't even clocked I'm there, too engrossed with what he's doing.

"Now, Jim, we have to remember we have company."

Lola's eyes point towards mine.

Looking my way, staring at me with eyes wide in panic, he stutters.

"H-h-hey, it's you. Shit. I didn't expect to see you here. Why are you here? I'm so sorry. How did you get in? I'm so sorry."

The bitch.

How could she?

Running out the front door, down the stairs, up the zig zag path and into the bushes to hide, a huge runner comes out of nowhere, nearly knocking into him as he shouts at me.

"You bloody lunatic, look where you're going."

All I see, hear, is Lola French kissing Jim, her mouth smirking, her eyes laughing at me.

I have to get away.

Unsee it.

Get away from them.

Finding a thick hedge, burying myself deep within it and crawling into a small space, the dirt underneath my fist's sprays in my face.

She knew how much I'd been looking forward to this.

She's my friend, isn't she?

The look on her face when she'd kissed him.

Is this why she'd asked about his gig?

Why couldn't she have just left him alone?

She has her pick of anyone, all she has to do is click her fingers and they come running. Why did she have to have Jim, too?

The front door slams, hearing her voice. Stiffening, fire rushes to my head ready to explode from all the thoughts.

"Jesse, Jesse."

Their feet pass me as they walk up the path.

Not moving an inch, trying to ignore my heart which has changed places with my brain, I listen.

"Jesse's always been a bit dramatic. All my life she's been jealous of me. It's a bloody joke. She's probably jealous of us. It happens all the time when guys like me. Just watch her, she'll probably try to steal you off me."

No.

Keeping completely still, waiting, not moving even an eyelid until they are past me, a little black bug with white spots crawls up my arm, grabbing it once their footsteps are out of ear range and throwing it as far as I can. Screaming inside, retching, not believing I'm dealing with this again. I really thought Lola had changed, turned a new leaf and grown up. I'd seen her do it to so many of her so-called friends at school. How could I have been so wrong to think she wouldn't do it to me?

I can't think straight, picking up a plastic cup close by and ripping it with my teeth, moulding it into a makeshift knife. Cutting into an old wound, watching the blood make patterns on the ground below, insects make their way to it and flies hover above, landing on my flesh. Flicking them away, trying to control my head from pinging off, I'm back at school with Lola and she's teasing me, hitting my face for fun.

The bitch.

Why couldn't she have just left him alone?

Suddenly hearing Celeste's voice, I want to run to her, but instead I sit and watch the blood flow.

"Jesse, are you here? Sorry I'm late. I was at the shops. Wait until you smell the bubble bath I got. Jim? Lola? What the hell are you two doing here? Where's Jesse?"

Chapter Seven

E yes moist, the thump of the base from the speakers slowly beats through my body as the lights of the club fade back in and a man's hand flicks in front of my face.

"You alright, love? Have you taken any drugs? Anyone in there?"

Swatting his hand away, glaring at him, sipping my drink, I can't believe I'm back here again with Lola about to take my second crush off me just because she can.

The red and green lasers above flick back and forth through my glass, watching them, ignoring everything around me until a high-pitched squeal to my left reminds me she's here, glaring at her, lifting my watered-down vodka to my lips watching her every move.

The glass vibrates against my teeth, retching as the gaggle of men surrounding her act like fools.

It's revolting.

Is she the only woman in the room?

She may as well be, other normal women don't have a shit show in hell against her.

The men, like puppy dogs, wait to see if they will be the lucky one she pets. The women, including me, want to rip her apart.

One of the men reminds me a little bit of Jim.

I wonder what he's doing now and if he ever did have any regrets about being lured away by her?

If he could only see her now. I wonder what he'd think.

I'm not sure he'd be so keen.

Would we still be together if he'd chosen me?

There's no use guessing. I'd never been given a chance with him or his dimples.

Greg's next song only adds to my overall mood. As if he knows what I'm thinking, *Taylor Dayne's 'Tell It to My Heart'* belts out while I mix my melted ice with the straw, sculling it back, spilling some water, wiping my wet leg.

Watching the pathetic scene before me, is Lola even my friend?

Celeste questions me daily about it, especially after finding her with Jim that day. She laid into her so much, they've hardly spoken since. Celeste's confused why I've chosen to still be friends with Lola saying any normal person would've dumped her ass and sent her on her way.

It's so complicated to explain.

I'm used to having Lola around.

It's been like that for so long, it's hard for me to break away. If I'm honest, the thought of losing her again scares me more than having her close. I've depended on her for almost everything my whole life. When we parted for those two years it was scary as hell, and weird.

Not normal.

I survived, and even made some friends, but in the back of my mind I always missed her, always felt a piece of the jigsaw was missing.

When she came back, so did my familiar, my normal.

My puzzle was complete.

We even managed to reconnect in a way that we hadn't before, but now I know it hadn't meant anything to her. I don't think she ever wanted to connect with me on a deeper level.

Watching her playing with the men around her now, she is very different to the girl I grew up with. At least as children the boys could either take or leave her, beauty not being the most important thing back then.

The woman standing before me now is far worse than the girl because she's way too aware of her beauty, more self-centred and entitled than ever. She'll never think about anyone but herself.

It doesn't take a rocket scientist to know what she's doing. I've even questioned God why He's wasted all the looks on someone so selfish?

I suppose it does come at a cost though.

The daily grief she suffers for it, no one sees that but me.

She doesn't have many friends and no one likes her much. She's had to show a different face to the world forever and keep whatever she feels inside hidden. No one really wants to know how she feels, even her parents.

I'm not sure I like her much these days, though. She'd dump me in a heartbeat if someone better came along, more compliant, less verbal.

Even the girls at The Orchard have told me to tell her to sling her hook, but when we're together, on our own, she has a way of turning situations into things they aren't. She makes my brain change the way it thinks; plants seeds into my head about people that grow until they take root and I eventually think of them the same way she does.

Now a lot of my friends have gone because Lola's fallen out with them. When she falls out with them she expects that I won't speak to them anymore, so they stop talking to me for nothing other than being Lola's friend.

It's isolating, like she doesn't want me to be friends with anyone but her. I'm beginning to see it clearer the more people have pointed it out.

But I still don't do anything about it.

The thought of letting her go, of being away from her again causes me too much anxiety.

I wish I knew why.

I really wish I could let her go.

Thump, thump, thump.

The bass and my heart combine, looking at the floor, deflated, defeated, deserted by the one person I thought would always be there.

"Jesse. Get me another drink. Jesse. Jesse. Get me another drink, *now*."

Slap

Burning, hearing skin on skin, a face that is anything but beautiful bends down into mine, flinching, shoving her hand away as her gorgeous grotesque face stares straight at me.

Was it a mistake finding her again?

Should I have just left her the fuck alone?

Looking towards the bar, the cute barman is watching, probably thinking I'm pathetic. Everyone does, me included. Flicking his head, winking at me, motioning me to the bar, I ask Lola what she wants even though I already know.

"You bloody know what I drink, you freak. Make it a double, and don't be so bloody long this time."

Pushing my way through the men lined up, bumping from one to the other like particles of gas, I make my way out to freedom and space staring back at the pathetic scene wondering why any of those men think they are special? None of them are. They're just little pawns in one of the many games Lola plays with people.

They'll learn.

Trudging towards the bar, confused with the attention from the barman, I'm guessing he probably wants to know about Lola.

I'm used to men approaching me to ask about her.

The bar is noisy, looking around awkwardly, seeing so many women all looking at the new barman.

How many has he summoned?

Watching him from the corner of my eye, *'Love Action'* by *The Human League* starts playing in the background, seeing me, ignoring everyone else and side stepping over to me with a smile.

"What can I get you to drink?"

I freeze.

"What's the matter? Cat got your tongue?"

Sweating, dizzy, counting the glasses in front of me, one, two, three, four, five, six, seven, eight, nine, ten, I'm calmer, answering, lowering my eyes to the bar.

"One d-double vodka & coke and one d-double Bailey's & i-i-ice, please?"

He notices my shaking hands.

"Which one's yours? Ice & a slice?"

"V-v-odka. Yes please, lime."

Why is he talking to me?

I don't understand.

Does he want to ask about drinks?

I don't get it.

Picking at the black polish on my nails, some of it rubs off on my left thumb.

"What's your name?"

"Why? No-one usually asks."

I'm nervous.

He knows it.

"It's J-J-Jesse."

Not looking at him, stuttering, I look back to Lola, suddenly feeling a hand tilt my head back around. He's staring straight into my eyes, both of us listening to the chorus of '*Love Action*' playing around us.

"Don't look around, then I can't see those beautiful eyes."

My face is on fire.

I don't know what to do.

The room starts spinning.

Looking up to the ceiling, breathing, twiddling my thumbs, looking down at the bar, I dare ask.

"W-w-what's your name?"

"Jayden, but people just call me J."

His eyes, fully focused on me, are giving me the creeps. He hasn't looked at Lola, asked me about her. No one ever looks at me over her. Why doesn't he want her?

Checking out his well-toned arms, he scratches his right arm giving me just enough time to see his tattoo. I just make out a red and green heart, and a name, and some numbers underneath.

Max 18.7.

Softly touching my scar on my left wrist tracing around the letters M. a. X, I cover up any other scars that might be visible. This has to be the sign I've been waiting for.

Who is his Max?

What does this mean?

Cutting a lime with his left hand, making a mental note to myself, I've always had a thing for left-handers. Not too tall, only about five-foot-eleven, he's perfect for my five-foot-five-inch frame.

A well-groomed black goatee beard and moustache suit his square face which has a touch of grey showing.

Smiling, winking at me, his cheeks look like they've been sprayed with lots of tiny light-brown dots of paint accentuating his rather wide nose. As he talks I see a tiny gap in his front teeth.

I haven't heard a thing.

Jet-black hair slicked back into a tiny ponytail looks very cool as does his body which is strong and fit, muscles bulging through his black trousers and black shirt, very similar to Joni's. A tiny tuft of dark chest hair pokes through his shirt seeing little droplets of sweat making their way down to his front button, which is undone, imagining running my fingers through it.

Looking down to his chest, grinning, his eyes stay focused, fixed on my face and lips. Uncomfortable and excited, something in those menacing dark eyes and the way he stares doesn't feel right.

Why?

Looking away, blushing, there are so many women in the room yet his eyes only see me?

Women everywhere point and smile wanting his attention, but

still he only sees me. Cleavages, butts, legs, beautiful faces. He ignores them all staying focused on me and only me.

This can't be happening.

I ignore my gut.

"Thanks."

"I hope to see you soon, beautiful."

Winking, quickly handing me a napkin, and serving the next person, I start walking back, unsteadily to the table, with the two double drinks, seeing the lime in my drink has been cut into a heart. My own heart somersaults in my chest.

Butterflies in my stomach, legs like jelly, return with the drinks. Lola quickly spots the lime in my vodka, ripping the napkin from my hand.

"Ring me? He gave you his number?"

"What? Did he?"

Wanting to rip the napkin from her hand, she suddenly announces we must go, grabbing her coat and charging out of the club while I stand, holding both drinks as men awkwardly stare at each other wondering what has happened.

I thought she'd be happy for me.

As the men quickly disperse, through them I see someone waving vigorously at me, nearly dropping my drinks.

Staring up at him, it can't be?

Surely not?

"Dimples?"

Smiling, walking towards me, Jim bends down and finds my cheek, kissing it.

Crack.

Electricity separates us, quickly snapping my head towards the bar seeing Jayden is watching Greg who's watching me. Stunned, wondering what on earth is happening, my mind is blank.

"Dimples?"

Our eyes meet.

The spark is still there. I'm back at Celeste's flat, opening the door, offering him my hand, but this time I offer him Lola's spare drink.

"A heart? Thanks."

Those dimples.

"Oops sorry, wrong drink."

Switching the two, he grimaces at the Bailey's, taking my arm to find a cosy spot for us to chat.

I'm in a dream.

This is not happening and soon I'll wake up.

Jayden's watching from the bar.

I smile.

Smiling back, he blows me a kiss.

When will I wake?

It's not a dream.

Lola's still here watching Jayden from the door, glaring. All I see is her mouth moving.

"You bastard."

Looking back at me she storms out, and Greg, who's also been watching from his DJ booth, quickly gives me the thumbs up as *Simple Minds* starts to play, '*Don't You Forget About Me.*'

Chapter Eight

"Faith is seeing light with your heart when all your eyes see is darkness."

— *Barbara Johnson*

HONK.

Six am, lying in bed, cursing the traffic for the hundredth time, a beam of sunlight sneaks through the curtains and bounces off some posters on my walls; I don't know how I'm going to concentrate today after the craziness of last night.

Beep, beep. Swish. Honk. Clunk.

The morning's city traffic is already building up.

Woof, woof, honk, meow.

Samantha?

On cue, a gentle meow at my bedroom door tells me she is safe, throwing back the covers and quickly scampering to the door to let her in. Jumping up onto my bed, taking her usual position, she curls up into a ball, running back to my bed to snuggle under the blankets grabbing her for my morning cuddle.

My room is lovely but not very warm. I wish it was better.

Kissing the top of her head, stroking her glossy soft fur, her hair tickles my mouth.

"What have you been up to this morning young lady?"

Meowing like she understands, tickling my cheeks with her wet nose, I'd love to know what she's thinking. Laying her head on her legs, curling into a ball, and closing her eyes, her purring sounds like a giant rattle in my ear.

Hardly sleeping a wink, every time my brain tried to switch off all it saw were images of Jayden, Jim, and my mother. It didn't help that I slunk in a little after two this morning, only just managing to change into my pyjamas, which I'm not surprised to see are on inside out. I hope Sharon didn't hear me? I remember collapsing on top of my bed and waking up freezing cold about an hour later.

I've never jumped under the blankets so fast.

I think I made myself a sandwich of some sort, but it might be my stomach telling me I'm hungry.

Licking my teeth, poking my finger into my mouth, I'm sure I taste remnants of cheese and vegemite, my favourite sandwich combo.

Meeting Jayden and Jim last night had completely taken me off guard. My gut is telling me to run as fast and as far away from Jayden as my legs will take me, but his eyes. They had the glint of the devil in them which I'm finding hard to resist.

Jim is obviously the better choice so why aren't I just choosing him?

"No one will ever want you, you ugly little bitch, not even God."

My mother's voice is always there to spoil any good thought I have.

Maybe she's right and I'm just clutching at straws with Jayden.

But what about Jim?

Can I trust him again?

Snuggling Samantha again, the fairytale in my head is real, wondering which one I'll end up with.

I'll prove my bitch mother wrong, and even if I don't end up with either of them, I'll find someone who will love me.

Rumbling loud behind my neck, Samantha's snoring fills my heart.

Stroking her fur, looking up to the ceiling and replaying the exact time mine and Jayden's eyes had connected, the intensity of his stare had made me feel like I was the only girl in the room.

I swear an electric charge had bolted all the way through my body causing shivers I couldn't explain.

It was like the music dulled around us and we were in our own little bubble.

I know I hadn't imagined it.

Had I?

The song.

If Greg had played it especially for me, then it'd definitely worked. 'Love Action' had made the moment almost too perfect catching eyes with Jayden almost as soon as the synthesised intro had started to play. If he'd jumped over the bar and taken me there and then I wouldn't have resisted.

Not that I knew anything about resisting anyone except the pervert from my past.

I hadn't even been kissed let alone made love to.

I'd only ever fantasised about it.

Slipping my hand below the covers, I find the right spot and close my eyes imagining him on top of me, inside me, kissing me, kissing every part of me. He licks me wherever he wants, loving being wanted, seduced.

Searching my brain for clues, anything, wanting too badly for everything I felt the night before to be real, he's with me in bed as 'Love Action' plays.

Flesh on flesh, his scent is all over me, on top of me, thrusting hard, looking into my eyes as I orgasm over and over, clutching the covers as I climax. Sitting up, breathing in and out deeply, my whole-body pulses, looking straight ahead, overcome with how powerful my body has responded.

Meow.

I didn't even feel Samantha get off the bed.

Laying back down, hand still below the covers, my fingers find the right spot again, rubbing, looking up at a black blob on the ceiling, rubbing, touching my breast, feeling its softness, imagining his lips on my nipple, sucking softly.

I want to know more about Jayden, desire to know if our stories are even remotely similar.

The darkness in his eyes excited me, made me curious to know more. His freckles, lips, cheeky grin.

His undivided attention to me.

Imagining his tongue inside me, licking between my legs, I taste my juices, smell my fingers, smell my lust.

Tasting sweeter than I expected, I wait for my breath to normalise, looking up to the black blob, asking.

"Am I imagining it? Does he really want me or is my need for love that obvious?"

He won't notice you next time you ugly little bitch! Who are you kidding?

Flicking the blankets over my head, trying to drown out my mother's voice, I hum 'Love Action,' hearing meowing at the door.

"In a minute, baby."

Why do I always let my bitch mother ruin my thoughts?

It's not like I don't know I'm letting myself get excited over something that will probably never happen. That Jayden was probably just being nice after seeing Lola slap my face and lap up all the attention.

Ok, he might've felt sorry for me, but was that really it? He might like me. It could be a possibility, couldn't it?

I won't let my mother's words win.

I'll go early next Wednesday night, tell Lola to meet me there at eleven instead of ten and see for myself whether he seeks me out, wants me alone?

Who am I kidding?

Pounding the mattress, I'm suddenly angry.

Why am I over analysing this so much?

I don't usually get so hot and bothered over a guy. I don't even like them much.

After Jim I'd all but given up.

But Jayden?

He isn't just any guy. I have a feeling this might go somewhere, despite what my gut is saying.

Surely my gut is panicking, steering me away from what might be the love of my life?

I thought that would be Jim.

Will I be lucky enough to get another go at it with Jayden?

Last night he'd been genuinely interested in me and for a teeny tiny second, I felt like the only woman in the club.

No-one but me and him, in our own little bubble.

Love Action.

Staring.

Wanting.

Just us.

Kicking the covers off, sitting up, my head feels ready to explode with all the thoughts bumping into each other. Both hands pulling my hair hard, yelling at the ceiling for some kind of clue, the black blob suddenly moves.

Oh God.

Samantha's seen it too and is looking up snarling from the door.

Carefully standing on top of my bed, spotting a tea towel on my side table, I flick at the spider with all the strength I have, terrified it might fall onto my head. Somehow connecting with it, it floats to the floor, its long black hairy legs scuttling straight towards Samantha and sudden death.

It has no chance.

Like a lamb to the slaughter, she pounces on it, sure I hear it screaming as she hunches, crunching it in her mouth.

That's not the kind of clue I was bloody looking for.

Flopping back down on my bed, waiting for my heartbeat to return to normal, Samantha sits by the door licking her mouth and my thoughts once again return to the previous night.

Do I ignore the signs?

The tattoo, the bubble, the eyes?

Rubbing my left wrist, staring at the letters, I know what my tattoo means.

What does his mean?

I'm so curious to know.

It's too much of a coincidence that we have the same name etched on our skin.

He has to be the one I've been waiting for.

Jim bolted as soon as Lola entered the equation. He chose her without a thought.

Jayden hadn't even given her a second glance.

Hadn't seen her.

I had to take notice of that and question it.

He couldn't *not* notice her.

Everybody did.

Bumping into Jim had definitely unsettled me. Of all the times to have seen him, did he know how much of a crush I'd had on him? Had Lola told him?

Why did he have to walk in the same night I met Jayden?

I'm so confused.

I'm glad Lola stormed out. I didn't need any reminder of what happened between them. Seeing them in the same place had definitely made me hurt a little.

I don't know whether I've fully forgiven her for deliberately stealing Jim away from me the way she did, but having decided to never speak about it again, I'd hoped the Cosmos would swallow it whole, absolutely never ever to be regurgitated again.

What the hell am I going to say to her now?

There's no way she'll ignore it, which means I'll have to talk about the whole sordid thing again, and that is something I really don't want to do.

I never thought I'd see Jim ever again.

What if I'd met him the week before? Would I be feeling differently about him now?

Would I even have looked Jayden's way?

This had to be the sign.

Shaking all the thoughts away, I'm cold, grabbing my dressing gown from behind the door and covering myself with its white, woolly warmth.

Watching my red and purple lava lamp beside my bed, Samantha's growling at the blobs of oil, suddenly diving onto the bed to touch it. Moving her away quickly, touching it with my finger, watching the squishy insides float around, I'm almost calm after my close call with the eight-legged freak.

Ouch. Calmness gone; I've forgotten how hot it is.

Full of bright colours, my bedroom is a place I feel comfortable being myself. I love anything colourful discovering it helps me feel better.

It's probably because my childhood was so dark.

Who knows?

I choose colour for almost everything, except when I'm picking something to wear. My mother's continual reference to me looking like the back end of a bus has made me gravitate towards a colour that makes my body look smaller.

Black was never going to be a colour I surrounded myself with, though.

Ever.

My set of drawers is a perfect example. Each drawer, painted a vivid red, yellow, orange, and blue, stands against the wall to the left of my bed. On top sit bottles of my favourite perfumes Ghost, Opium and Alien and next to them sit a baby spider plant and jade jewellery box I bought from a second-hand shop. Full of beaded necklaces, hooped earrings, and bangles, all of which I hardly wear, the girls gave them to me hoping I might somehow become more 'girly.' I've never really worn any jewellery, finding it a nuisance to put on.

A multicoloured striped runner given to me by Celeste clashes badly with the colours of the drawers, but that's what makes me like it more. A silver-framed picture of Gail takes pride of place in the middle.

Smiling at me with her beautiful smile, picking it up I kiss her, stroking her face like she's still here with me. Every line of her weathered skin visible in the morning light, my eyes moisten, brushing her face with my finger tip.

"We're all a bit broken, baby girl. Some of us more than others. Show them what you got. Find your wings and show the world how special you are."

She used to tell me everyone was broken one way or the other, that she was until I came along. 'My heart was broken, baby girl. You fixed it, you mended my heart.'

I'd do anything to hear her voice again.

My life would be so different if she were still here.

Why couldn't God have taken my mother and left Gail here with people who loved her?

Placing the picture back down and making my way towards Samantha, who's meowing at the door, I catch my foot on the fluffy light-brown round rug in the centre of the room, hanging onto the door for dear life to stop myself falling. I added the rug to bring a little softness to all the right angles of the furniture.

I think every room needs something round.

Posters of people I adore pout, snarl, and smile down at me from every wall. One of many women I love covers an entire space. Magazine cuttings, posters, and articles I've ripped from newspapers show Madonna's versatility and uniqueness in an industry dominated by men. Hair teased to an inch of its life or styled into a bouffant or side ponytail always make her look stylish.

I personally adore the bouffant but would never try it on myself.

I'd never look as good.

Crucifixes, black plastic bangles all the way up both arms, off-the-shoulder crop-tops and miniskirts in all different colours; she looks gorgeous. Huge, hooped earrings, fishnet tights and gloves, lace leggings, shoes, and boots; the ever-present plunging cleavage, shows she is ballsy, confident, and strong.

I'm going to be like her one day.

Drawn to a poster of her dressed in a white wedding gown, pouting with her fingertip sitting on her deep red bottom lip, she's definitely no saint.

Trying to sing like her, pointing at the poster, my voice is still a little husky from last night, pretending she can hear me.

"God I hope Jayden's touch is as good as in the song."

Wondering if Jayden and Jim would like my room, I scoop Samantha up carrying her to the bed to grab the tea towel I used to flick the spider off the ceiling with. Deducing I must have made myself something to eat last night, there are smears of vegemite all over it.

I hope I enjoyed it.

Letting Samantha out, shutting the door again and spinning around to grab my slippers, Saffron from Republica snarls at me from the space above my drawers. I love her dyed-black bob and stunning bright-red around the edges. It suits her beautiful sneery face as does Siouxie Sioux's jet-black hair, another idol of mine snarling from the left of Saffron.

No one is as cool as Siouxie, not even Madonna.

Touching my own hair, dyed the same vivid-red on the ends as Saffron's, I don't look anywhere near as beautiful.

Blowing a kiss to George Michael right next to them, I remember ripping the poster out of a magazine waiting to see the doctor. So many eyes had judged me that day, but I couldn't resist his ever so tiny white shorts and gorgeous legs. I love loads of Wham's songs and I love him, although I know men are probably kissing those glorious lips.

Looking across to my favourite poster, I'm in love. Adam Ant stands gazing at me in his military jacket. Two, big, thick red stripes across his right cheekbone border one white stripe through the middle making him look almost tribal. His dreamy purple eye-shadowed eyes stare fixedly at me and a tiny red heart above his left eyebrow winks, teasing me. A black mole to the left of his nose looks fake, but I don't care. Grabbing his left elbow with his right hand, his left thumb points to his ruby shiny lips as his right arched eyebrow lures you in. I've fantasised about marrying my Prince Charming for years.

That is, until this morning.

Drop dead gorgeous, I've had the biggest crush on Adam Ant for as long as I can remember after browsing the 80's section of a record shop one day. Finding the album, I'd instantly fallen in love not caring what he sounded like. I now know every word to every song.

Touching his lips with mine, giving him a smooch, "Too late, Adam, I'm now taken. We could have had such beautiful babies."

I was definitely born in the wrong era, identifying with the 80's more than any other decade. I simply love the music and fashion that went with it, and Adam Ant, who's probably way past it now, is the biggest reason why.

Pinching myself at my good luck at being given the whole of the downstairs at The Orchard, Sharon had allowed me to decorate it as I please.

"No painting murals on my walls or too bright colours, Ok?"

Sharon had warned me not to go overboard.

I'd ignored her.

The biggest room, my bedroom, is parallel from the next biggest, the sitting room. The two remaining, a small mustard-coloured kitchen, and the bathroom, minimal with only an avocado-green bath, sink and toilet, haven't been decorated at all.

Some of the girls helped me paint the lounge walls red and magnolia, donating almost everything I needed in the way of furniture.

Celeste personally feng shui-ed my space and gave me a beautiful tapestry for my lounge as well as a number of cuttings from her beautiful plants. Two rock salt lamps at each end of the sofa, also donated by her, add beautiful soft lighting, creating an ambience of calm and tranquillity to either read, draw, or listen to my music.

Walking from the bathroom to the kitchen, quickly filling the kettle for a much-needed coffee, I spot bread, butter, cheese, and vegemite all over the worktop seeing I didn't even put the top back on the vegemite. Or the butter back in the fridge.

Cleaning the crumbs and mess away, Samantha has followed me, meowing as I scoop up her crusty bowl of old food and throw whatever's left inside in the bin. The smell and consistency of the new pouch of food makes me retch, placing it on the floor, quickly pouring myself a coffee walking through to the lounge, resting my warm cup on the table. My 'Salt-N-Pepa' album stares at me from the couch, picking it up and making sure there are no scratches or fur on it.

Returning it to its sleeve, Samantha busies herself at the door grooming her fur after eating her food, stretching, and jumping onto the couch beside me. Laying down to absorb the sun on her beautiful silver tabby coat, meowing up at me, I tell her to be careful with my records, lifting and hugging her close to my cheek. Tickling my lips with her fur, rubbing cheeks, she jumps from my arms and makes her way to the litter box.

"Great."

Looking around, I still have a lot of work to do in this room.

One tatty couch covered with a red throw has arms that look like they've seen better days. Gouged-out chunks of foam on the arms are an eyesore, but I can't complain, I'd been given it for free from another one of the girls.

Making a mental note to try to get some sort of cover for the arms, the tapestry Celeste surprised me with smiles from the back wall. Black and white, the huge sun is enough to decorate the entire wall and looks wonderful against the red colour of the paint. Celeste has such an eye for decorating, always advising me on different ways to move furniture around to give the room a bit more space.

Five plants on my window sill lap up the morning sun, each magnificent in their own way. My favourite, the Indian Hoya, is growing longer by the day, each of its ropes intertwined with light and dark-green foliage, the pink waxy flowers adding to its beautifulness. Grown from a tiny cutting, I'm so proud of how it's grown. The male and female spider plants have produced babies, the female with her string of four babies, positively blooms with motherly pride. The male, resplendent as a peacock and obviously very happy in the old, cracked flower teapot I've used to plant him in, sits next to her. Both losing colour, it bothers me, moving them from the window, positioning them on the coffee table out of the direct sunlight hoping that might help. One of the leaves lands in my coffee, quickly scooping it out, rubbing the warm liquid off hoping it hasn't harmed it in any way.

My Jade plant, unfortunately refuses to thrive. Trying different soil and many contrasting pots, a tatty pink cheap iron tin doesn't look like the right environment either.

I won't give up.

My plants are like babies to me, loving them all, especially my sunflowers which bow to their sun god, grateful for the warmth. The lavender I picked from my last walk infuses the air with its familiar scent. In a long yellow vase, the purple flowers look striking against the vase's hue.

My pièce de resistance, my record player, purchased from another charity shop, takes pride of place right opposite the couch along the wall. Sat on top of a cheap white wooden unit with twelve square hollows perfect for records, the speakers sit either side of the turntable. A dull-brown runner along the top of the unit, thanks also to Celeste, hides a multitude of scratches on the wood.

I've spent many nights listening to my music, a means of escape I can't resist. My record collection, all purchased from charity shops, is growing.

Bowie, Neneh Cherry, Bob Dylan, Joni Mitchell, Marianne Faithful, Tom Waits, Jimi Hendrix, Depeche Mode, Fleetwood Mac,

Tracy Chapman, Ian Dury, Voice of the Beehive, Aretha, Siouxie, Ella, Salt-N-Pepa, Beastie Boys, Mama's & the Papa's, Kate Bush, Pink Floyd, Public Enemy, Whitney, and even a bit of Kylie, a guilty pleasure I don't admit to often. There is a little bit of my soul in all of them, identifying with many of the lyrics. Placing Salt-N-Pepa back in its rightful spot, flicking through my records choosing 'Rumours,' I dust it off positioning it on the turntable. Lowering the needle, waiting for the crackle, I remember the first time I heard it...

Chapter Nine

"You're not broken. Someone who didn't love you convinced you that you are."

— *Unknown*

28th July 1986—I am ten

The noises won't rub away.

I've tried, but the animal clawing at me from inside is making my tummy hurt. I haven't eaten today so that's probably why. Now I have to walk home because Mother won't pay for a bus pass. On my birthday, too. She doesn't care.

Walking past bins, slyly looking inside, I find a half-eaten burger and chips still warm in its paper bag unsure if it's warm from the sun or because someone's just thrown it away, but I don't care.

I've never eaten a hamburger ever.

A half-drunk warm coke I've found next to them washes the foul fatty food down, waiting for the bubbles to come to my nose, but nothing happens.

I always eat food so fast when I'm starving. I'm afraid it'll be taken away or I'll lose it somehow. Bits of the burger are stuck half way down to my stomach and aren't moving.

I know why.

It's happened before when I've eaten fast.

Bending, face in the bin in case I vomit, the old grease and fat on my tongue swirls around in my stomach while the flies fly in and out and around my face. The smell makes the lump want to come up fast; a lady walking past stops to ask if I'm okay, but I don't answer her in case I'm sick all over her.

She doesn't care.

She probably thinks I'm just another dumb kid living in a rough neighbourhood.

I'm not stupid.

Zoe, my best friend, calls me dumb all the time. She'd call me dumb if she saw me now.

She doesn't know I haven't eaten for days. I haven't told her because she might tell someone, and then I might get taken away again and I don't want that to happen.

Mother is on another trip.

It doesn't usually happen in school time so whatever it is, it must be important.

I hate it when I have to find food in bins, but what else can I do? I've been on my own loads of times before but Mother usually leaves me something to eat. She didn't leave anything this time.

I have to make sure no one sees me taking food out of the bins because they'll call someone to check on me again. I sat in the dark, terrified, waiting for them to leave the last time they came. I'm sure they knocked for five hours.

Mother leaves the cupboards and freezer locked when she goes. If I'm lucky I'll find a handful of rotten fruit or a stale packet of biscuits on the table when I get home, but they don't usually even last a day.

I wonder if she'll be home today.

I want to see her, but I hope she's been found dead somewhere too.

Lifting my head out of the bin, quickly crossing myself in case God thinks my thoughts are mean and tells the devil to come take my soul, I don't want to go to hell, hitting myself over the head to show God how sorry I am for thinking bad thoughts. Hopefully He'll forgive me just this once.

Passing the corner shop, quickly looking around the back to see if the big black bins have been emptied, I sneak in through a little slit and hop up onto a red plastic box used to store bottles. Looking inside the big, gigantic black metal box, it stinks of rotting food and stale smells and I have to hold my nose closed with my fingers. Spotting a few loaves of bread, a whole cake, and a bag of very ripe bananas, I scoop them up running back through the slit sprinting away before the shopkeeper sees me.

He's caught me before and yelled at me, but he's never managed to catch me.

He's way too old.

I don't know why he yells at me.

The food is in the bin so why can't he just be nice and let me have it?

Stealing or finding what I can until my mother decides I've been punished enough for something I don't know I've done; I wish I knew what it was, then I could tell God I'm sorry and she'd come back and look after me.

Taking a big bite out of the coconut cake topping, it's gooey on my tongue and a little stale.

I've had way worse before.

Eating until the sugar makes me dizzy, I hate the way my stomach won't let me eat anymore. It knows how hungry I am.

Turning into my street, a car I haven't seen before is parked right outside my house. Slowing down, wiping my mouth with my sleeve, and taking a better look while I put the food I have inside my school-bag. I'm not sure whether to walk around the block again just to see if the car goes but, like a nosey cat, I walk up the three steps to my house, very slowly, placing both hands on the dirty glass of the window to block out the light and peer inside.

It's a bit hard to see through the dirty, grey, ripped net curtains, but I think I see someone moving.

Is Mother home?

The last time she came home I had to run to the park to hide because she wouldn't stop hitting me.

I don't want to do that again.

I don't like the dark.

There's never anywhere warm to hide and the noises scare me.

At least I've already found some food if that happens again.

Whoever's inside has seen me, opened the door and is welcoming me in before I can do anything about it.

An ugly skinny woman with a thin smile and cheekbones that could cut my cake stands staring at me. How did she get in? She's probably been told about me by the school again and they've given her the keys to come and get me. It's happened before. I try so hard at school not to look poor and crazy, but it's hard, especially when my mother cuts my hair.

The ugly skinny woman looks me up and down with her huge bulging eyes that look like a frog.

Who is she?

Where is Mother?

Pushing me in, closing the door behind me and walking to a small, tanned, round man with dark stringy hair that tries to hide a little bald patch on top of his head, his face looks like a tomato, ruby, red and round.

I wonder if I squish it whether his brains will spurt out of his eyes?

An old brown suitcase at his feet tells me they are ready to take me away.

Here we go again.

The woman tells me my mother needs another 'little rest' which means she's back in the hospital.

No wonder she hasn't been home.

Their sad eyes look at me and then around the filthy lounge towards the arms of the couch behind them which I've pulled the insides out of. The woman grabs my wrist staring at the letters etched on my skin, asking what I've done.

I won't tell her I tried giving myself a tattoo ages ago. I haven't done it again, but I still cut myself.

It makes me feel better.

Her huge, brown, bulgy eyes stare at me under her short brown curls; hollow cheeks make her look a lot older for someone I guess is younger than I think.

The light-brown flowery dress she has on doesn't fit her properly hiding what looks like a skeleton holding her up. She sort've blends in with the couch behind her. Her thick, black tights and clumpy black shoes with a little heel on, don't.

They don't even look like they belong on her bony body at all.

Her skin, a funny yellow, has patches of brown all over it with scars that I can still see underneath the tons of makeup she's using to try to hide them. The makeup doesn't work because I can see the black rings under her eyes too. Lots of tiny soft hair covering her face is visible through the light coming in from the window; I have to stop myself from stroking it.

All of a sudden, her thin lips start to move and straight away I think a lizard tongue will come out and bite me. Flinching, listening to her deep voice, which sounds like a robot, she promises me that the family I'm going to are ready and excited to meet me.

Great, just some more strangers to pretend there's nothing wrong in my life.

I wonder what these ones will be like.

The older looking man standing with the ugly thin woman has big blue eyes that turn down which look like they might start crying at any minute. Maybe it's because his suit is too big.

I'm confused.

Why are he and the ugly thin woman both wearing clothes that don't fit them?

Picking up my suitcase and leading me to the car outside, I follow his hairy hands full of brown spots.

Guiding me to the same car I didn't recognise, an old brown Citroen Tesla, I wait for it to be unlocked. Sad, panicking, wondering whether this family will be different, will they have any kids of their own?

I like it better when they don't because it means I won't have to fight with anyone.

Most of the families' kids hate me.

I know that because they always look at me in a horrible way.

I usually end up being bullied, or touched.

I don't say anything because no one will believe me.

I've been to enough places now to tell when they don't want me there.

Feeling like my head might burst, I'm afraid I won't fit in the car, but the ugly skinny woman pushes me in and I know it's not the size of a balloon because it fits just fine.

Sliding in next to me while the driver puts my suitcase in the boot, the ugly thin woman keeps touching her nose and sniffing loudly. I know why and don't care. I'm used to all the names and the way people look at me.

Her robot voice, which sounds like a man, suddenly says words I don't understand.

"There's a bit of an atmospheric condition in here. Would you mind opening the window?"

I'm guessing she thinks I stink. I know I'm right because she starts coughing and waving her hand over her nose. Up close she's even more thin and ugly. I'm scared of her darting eyes which look like they have springs in the back of them. The blacks of her eyes are slits. She looks even more like a lizard than before.

She's a lizard with patchy flaky skin.

I'm sure she'll show me a lizard tongue soon.

The fuzz on her face up close is thick, clumped together with the clay-like orange make-up and her hands look too big for her body. All her fingernails are bitten and the ends of her fingers look like they have scales on them.

The skin is so thick.

Is she a lizard trapped in a human?

Looking away, I've already started ignoring her, instead gazing out the window concentrating on anything other than what she's saying. I have no idea what I'm in for; watching the trees that go on forever melt into one making it look like a very long wall.

Trapped, my mind starts asking the same questions it always asks when I go to a new house.

Will I still be going to the same school?

How will I tell Zoe, my best friend, if I'm not?

Will the family be nice or will they look at me with the same eyes nearly every family has looked at me with?

The families all pretend to care, but I know they just feel sorry for me. Zoe will know if I don't come to school that something is up. I'm sad it's happened now because I was feeling good, feeling happier.

This always happens when I start feeling better.

I was only thinking the other day how my mother hadn't been away for such a long time. I thought she was fixed, that I would never have to go away again.

Why?

Why did it have to happen again?

I hate her more than anything. I wish she was dead, then maybe I could live somewhere with people who don't treat me like an animal.

Why does she keep coming back?

Why do they keep sending me back to her?

Quickly crossing myself, saying sorry to God again in my head, trying not to think about her dying, I hum a song to stop asking myself more questions. The ugly thin woman sees me and glares.

I glare back humming louder.

How long will I have to stay at this place?

I never get enough time to prepare for it.

It's the same every time.

I come home and my bags are always packed ready to go.

Why do they keep thinking I'm ok with this?

Scratching my skin, dirty sharp chewed nails dig into my flesh, scratching, scratching, scratching, humming, nervous about where I'm going.

Is it real or am I just dreaming because I'm so hungry?

Cough, cough.

It's real.

The ugly woman asks me again to open the window.

Ignoring her, I listen to cars beeping, motorcycles zooming, trucks honking and cyclists' bells tinging.

Can they see me?

Do they know I want to jump out the window and run anywhere I can?

Scratching my head, I know my hair stinks. I can smell it, smell myself. I haven't washed for days or changed my clothes because all my other clothes are either dirty or growing mould piled up in a corner of my bedroom.

It adds more smells to my already smelly house.

I'm so used to smelling bad, I don't notice it much anymore.

The kids at school do.

Their favourite name for me is Ronstink.

Coughing, the ugly thin woman bends across me, winding down the window, grabbing my hand asking me to desist from scratching my head.

What does desist mean?

She's looking at me like I'm some kind of animal and talking to me in a language I don't understand.

Glaring at her, winding the window back up, I hate her, scratching my arm instead of my head.

Her lizard eyes aren't friendly at all.

She's just another adult for me not to trust, to dislike, or despise.

I know what those words mean because we've been learning them at school and had to look up the word hate.

I'm glad I did.

Looking at me through the mirror, the driver winks at me. I like him. He understands the way I'm feeling more than the stick insect sitting next to me. His funny face makes me forget where I'm going for a tiny second.

Where am I going?

The ugly thin woman sits stiff as a post next to me, hands clenched over her knees, glaring at me sideways, eyes bulging out of her skull. Lips pursed, handing me a tissue for my skin, she gestures with her hand to wipe.

I don't.

I just stare at her.

Half an hour later, driving down a few winding streets, I feel sick as we finally arrive. Stepping out of the car, a huge double-storeyed mansion surrounded by trees is so different from where I live, I'm not sure it's real. I'm told it's a one-acre property in the rich part of the Kapiti Coast.

I don't even know where the Kapiti Coast is.

No other families' houses I've ever been to have looked like this.

Mouth hanging down to the ground, it's suddenly closed shut by the thin ugly woman who pushes me away from the car door and up the stairs to where the family are ready to greet me.

Regular mum, dad and two grown up sons, the Quinn's wait for me at the door. Mum (Ava) is short and curvy with big, rounded black glasses that don't suit short cropped light brown hair. Little beady dark brown eyes too close together make her look like a cartoon. Her long nose and thin stiff lips don't match her full body either, but I decide she looks like a little mouse all dressed up, only needing whiskers to finish the look off.

Wearing clean white trousers and a t-shirt with lots of different sized colourful flowers, she smells of a scent I don't know. I like it. Smiling at me, showing two big front teeth, now I really do think she looks like a mouse as she steps forward to give me a big hug. Flinching, stiffening, expecting to be hit, I think she's going to cry, but she gently pats me on the shoulder looking at me with concerned eyes, telling me not to worry.

Dad (John) is tall, skinny and wears glasses too. Thick round frames make his eyes look teeny tiny and his long face, lengthy nose that looks like it might grow, thin lips, light blue eyes, and wrinkles on his forehead and around his eyes make him look old.

I don't think he is old.

Maybe it's because he's so thin, like the ugly woman, that I think that.

He has a dark chin, like someone has painted grey on it, but it suits him. It's patchy grey in places and darker, like it's been blobbed on with a paintbrush. Wearing plain grey tracksuit bottoms and a t-shirt with words 'The Who' on it, his open sandals show long yellow toenails and crusty feet.

Yuk.

Stepping in to give me a hug, flinching again, he doesn't know what to do. Eyes wide, not blinking at each other, he steps back and I find the driver, standing beside him, feeling his protective hand on my shoulder.

I like Ava and John.

They have kind eyes.

The two sons Anton (twenty-three) and Bradley (twenty) who I later discover are both at University in Palmerston North, have come to meet me too and stand beside their parents.

Bradley definitely doesn't want me there.

His dark-blue eyes have lots of darkness underneath them, like he hasn't slept for days; his mouth looks like an upside-down smile.

Folded arms let me know loud and clear he doesn't like me or want me anywhere near the place.

Just another one to add to the list.

Anton, the older brother, seems friendlier. His eyes smile. Wavy thick blonde hair that sticks to the side of his head hangs to his shoulders and his round black glasses, like his dad's, make his dark-brown eyes look small. Eyes like his mum's, he's tall and tanned, like a surfer, and wears a black t-shirt with the words '*Black Sabbath*' on it with pictures of men who stare at me from his chest.

I already like him.

His brother, a lot smaller, doesn't wear glasses like the others. His dark-blonde hair seems thicker, more like grass growing from his head. It's straight and flat at the top like someone has got a lawnmower and cut straight across it. He's still scowling, glaring at me, shoulders up, arms folded, stiff like a cat that's ready to pounce on a mouse which isn't making me feel safe.

He doesn't look like the rest of the family.

He doesn't even look related.

Staying close to the driver, we all go inside not even given the choice as the ugly thin woman pushes me from behind. Wrapping his hands around my shoulders and gently patting me, the driver bends down, whispering in my ear.

"Don't worry, little lady. It'll be alright. Be strong and remember, it's only for six weeks and then you'll be home again."

Six weeks.

Home again?

I don't want to go back to my mother.

She's crazy and doesn't treat me nice.

Don't they all know that?

Scratching my arms, I don't see the blood, but the ugly thin woman does handing me another tissue. She's not making it any easier for me. I wish she'd just go outside and wait in the car and leave me with the driver. Ava comes close to me and tries to take my hand, but I flinch and she steps back.

I want to run.

I can't because I know I'll get into lots of trouble.

Bradley shouts.

"What's that smell? It's disgusting."

I know what he's thinking.

His eyes tell me.

I hate him.

I can't hold it in anymore; my eyes start pouring. Ava and the driver try to hug me but it's all too much. The ugly thin woman stands stiff and Anton and John look at Bradley telling him off with their eyes.

He doesn't care.

He's just like all the other children who hate me.

The other children are usually a lot younger though, not in their twenties.

Taking lots of breaths, I feel so dizzy, humming a song, rocking back and forth while Ava shoves a brown paper bag under my mouth telling me to blow into it.

I'm glad she's here.

Asking to go to the toilet she shows me where it is, hearing them talking about me as I go.

I know what I have to do to get through the next six weeks. I don't want to be here but I do, as well.

Splashing water on my face, breathing in and out, I go back out and do what I have to do.

Staying close to the driver as we look around the house, I've never seen anything like it. I didn't notice it before but everything smells of Ava. Spotless, there's no dust, dirt, or mould anywhere.

It's so different from what I'm used to living at home.

Square, red cushions sit on brown leather couches and the furniture is shiny, even seeing my face in some of the tables. The carpet is stain free and there's no piss stains or cigarette marks anywhere. Something on top of a large dark wooden cabinet catches my eye wanting to see it up close. Encased in glass, sitting on what looks like a gold candlestick holder is an egg painted with lots of beautiful flowers. Red, purple, yellow, and orange, each flower's petals are so perfect that I could reach up and pick them off and smell them. On top of the red flower sits a butterfly so real I think it might fly down and land on my hand.

Following my gaze, everyone looks up very soon hearing Ava's voice.

"Do you like that, Jesse? Beautiful isn't it? It's very special to us. An heirloom. Do you know what that is?"

I shake my head to let her know I don't.

"John's family from a long time ago handed it to his great, great, great, grandmother. She came from Russia and that's what they used to give each other for Easter back then. It's been protected for all this time and he's the one who it was handed down to being the oldest child. It'll go to one of our boys one day and then one of their children. It's real inside. Imagine? That's why we have to protect it, the shell is so fragile."

Smiling at Ava, nodding, moving towards the heirloom to pick it up, my arm can't reach. I want to see it, want to hold it in my hand to see how it feels.

"No, Jesse, I'm afraid you can't hold it. No one can, it's too fragile. That's why we keep it up there. You can look at it but please don't ever touch it, ok?"

Sad, I want to see it up close but do as I'm told because everyone is watching me. Suddenly shoved towards the kitchen I spot a bowl of fruit.

Why isn't anything locked up?

Bananas, apples, and pears smile at me from the bowl on the kitchen table, grabbing three bananas, greedily peeling, and eating them before anyone can take them off me. Chomping, chewing so fast I think I might choke; these bananas aren't like the ones at home. These are fresh and hard and yellow.

"Now, Jesse, there's plenty of fruit for you to eat whenever you want. You'll spoil your appetite for dinner if you eat too much."

This is my dinner, doesn't Ava know.

Pushed again towards a side table, mouth bulging, I look at happy pictures of the boys at different ages smiling, some with missing teeth.

Wondering whether their teeth were pulled out with pliers like mine, a tiny photograph tucked behind one of the photos catches my eye. Picking it up, swallowing some banana, I point at it, asking.

"Who's she?"

Ava's voice cracks, breathing in.

"That's my niece. We hardly see her."

Looking at the photograph, I think she looks friendly, like someone I know but I can't remember who.

"That's sad. What's her name?"

"Maxine, but we just call her Max. I think she's around the same age as you, Jesse. I'd forgotten that was there."

Taking the photograph from my hand, she rubs the girl's face and for a tiny second, I think I've heard that name before.

Rubbing my wrist, trying to remember where I've seen her, the banana peel falls from my hand to the floor, picking it up, staring at the name etched on my wrist.

It was probably the worst pain I'd ever experienced in my life...

One year before...

... I'm alone at home again. I've been here for five days now and don't know when my mother is coming back.

I'm scared and hungry all the time.

I never feel safe when I'm on my own. There's no grown up to help me with anything. I'm not allowed to leave the house because Mother said if I do I might be taken away or followed, or I might be hurt by bad people who live near us. The noises I hear outside at night scare me, so I know she's telling the truth. She's left lots of times before, usually for a couple of days but never more than five. I don't know if she'll be back this time. It feels different. I don't know where she goes or why it's always during the holidays, but I always know when she's going to leave because she starts putting food on the table and tells me not to touch it.

It's always the same.

It's the Easter holidays now and she knows I'm off for two weeks. Maybe that's why she's gone for longer?

It's so boring.

I get bored a lot and usually just stay in the sitting room until she gets home. I never leave the lights on in case someone comes to the door. I close the curtains and just sit in the dark until the sun goes to sleep and I can turn on a lamp or the telly to keep me company. I sometimes find spiders or other bugs on the piles of clothes I use to cover me and that can be fun.

One time I even found a mouse but my mother killed it when I told her.

I was really sad and thought I'd done something bad by telling her.

I felt so sad for the mouse when I saw it in the trap.

I've never seen one again. I think my mother has put traps around the house to stop them coming in. Our house is dirty all the time so I can see why the bugs and mice like it.

I don't.

I can't remember ever seeing my mother clean. I don't think she minds being dirty. I don't think she minds me being dirty either. I know that because when she's here I have to empty her bucket beside her bed. She said she can't go to the toilet properly. I'm glad when she goes because I don't have to do that.

That's something I hate doing.

Tonight I'm watching a programme on telly called Crimewatch and there's something about a girl who's been missing for a long time. I'm not usually allowed to watch the telly, especially things like this. They found a body in the woods and it's scary to watch, but I can't stop watching it. The music scared me at first but I've kept watching it because something inside my brain really wants to.

I can't explain it.

The police say they're going to reopen something. I don't understand it but they want to know if it was suicide or murder. I think suicide means they killed themselves. I'm not sure. I don't know how people can be so evil.

They remind me a lot of my mother.

I think I might see her on Crimewatch soon.

If people are so evil surely God will punish them?

The girl who went missing had a funny mark on her shoulder, a red and green tattoo.

I remember watching a song about a girl with a red and green tattoo. The girl in the song was called Maxine.

I wonder if it's the same girl they're looking for?

Anyway, I love the tattoo of the woman so I've decided I want one just the same. I'm going to do it myself with a sharp knife. They showed her tattoo close up so I drew it and have decided it's way too hard so I'll just tattoo the name of the girl in the song on my wrist instead. I won't tattoo her whole name, just Max will do. I hope the girl in the song likes it. I'm going to use a knife and ink from my fountain pen. I'm sure it won't be that hard. I've seen on tv how they scratch something sharp onto people's skin and then put ink into the veins. The girl they're looking for looks like someone I know, but I don't remember who.

I don't know if I should know her.

I don't think so but maybe I should.

It's her eyes.

They are nearly the same colour as my best friend Zoe's.

Maybe that's it.

Grabbing the sharpest knife, I can find; I get ready and give myself a tiny scratch to see how it feels.

I'm nervous.

In front of the telly with the knife on my wrist, will it hurt more than the other times I've cut myself? I hope not but I'm sort've excited to see if it does. I haven't felt much over the last five days, mostly nothing. I've asked God to make the emptiness go away but He hasn't listened to me.

He never listens to me.

Seeing the woman is a sign for me to feel, I know it.

Placing the end of the knife on my left wrist slowly cutting into my skin, it hurts.

My skin turns red, redder than I thought it would be. I've never cut my wrist before, only my legs and sometimes my arms. The blood keeps coming from where I've cut. It's only a small cut, and I don't know why, but I keep on cutting; but I don't go near the veins because the tattooist on the show I watched said not to go near them.

My skin feels hot.

The more I cut, the redder it gets, but I don't stop. I must be someone else because I didn't think I would have the guts to do it.

M a X.

My insides scream for me to stop.

Breathing hard, looking at the knife, there's blood all over it.

I'm sure there wasn't this much blood on the show I watched.

Maybe there was.

All my fingers and my wrist are red too, looking at what I've done, opening up the little cuts to see how deep I've cut. They're only small, but there's lots of blood. Squeezing ink from my fountain pen onto my skin, it stings.

Throwing the knife across the room, my brain goes all dizzy and my eyes shut.

I don't know how long my eyes shut, but when I wake the blood is crusty and blue and my wrist burns with pain.

I don't know what to do.

I'm scared.

My wrist hurts.

I think I'm going to die.

Why did I do it?

"Mother, where are you? I'm scared."

Bang.

Outside it sounds like a car has shot someone because I hear a woman scream. I'm frightened they might come and get me.

Quickly finding a rag to tie around my wrist, I try to remember how the people I've seen on television stopped the blood. Wrapping the rag around my wrist I hold it tight humming a song.

I feel better, lighter.

When I think about my mother it feels easier.

Three days later Mother comes home and doesn't notice anything. I even have the bandage still wrapped around my wrist and it has blood on it.

She doesn't see it.

I don't think she wants to see it because if she did then I'd know she'd care about me and I know she doesn't.

No-one does.

No-one ever asks how I am, not even God.

"You little bitch, go and make me a cup of tea."

Chapter Ten

"Dear music,

Thanks for always clearing my head,

healing my heart, and lifting my spirits."

— *Lori Deschene*

I feel sad.

Looking down at my bumpy skin, rubbing it, side stepping away from Ava, who is still staring at the photograph of the girl, I really hope she doesn't ask me about my M a X on my wrist because I'll have to tell her about that night.

I won't like that.

I can't remember when I started cutting myself. It was a mistake but I found that it made me feel good. I remember feeling strange because I liked it and I knew I shouldn't. It made me feel that whatever bad things my mother was doing to me there was something I could do to make me feel better.

She doesn't know I do it.

I've got lots of scars, a lot from when she ties me up in the chair, but the new scars I hide with my clothes so nobody can see them, especially the teachers. They'd send me away if they could so I cut places that my clothes will hide them.

I like to feel the bobbly skin through my clothes.

I don't know why that makes me feel better, but it does.

When I feel like I want to explode, which is quite a lot, I go to my room or out the back and cut myself and then I feel better.

I don't know how I'm going to be able to do it here at Ava's.

I'll have to sneak something in and do it at night when they can't see.

Standing next to the thin ugly social worker, rubbing my leg through my clothes, I wait until Ava is finished looking at the picture to ask if Maxine has any brothers or sisters?

"Yes, one brother."

"Why haven't you got any pictures of him?"

"We just don't. Something happened and we don't like to talk about it. Best you just leave it, Jesse. It was lucky his mother even sent me a picture of Maxine. I would love to meet her."

Nudging me in the back, the ugly thin woman asks if she can show me where I will be sleeping.

I think that's the only good thing she's said today.

Carefully replacing the photograph of the girl, I think I see two tiny tears racing down Ava's cheeks, but I'm not completely sure. Smiling, wiping her face, Ava's sad eyes take me and the ugly thin woman whose name I now know is Ethel, into what will be my bedroom for the next six weeks. Leaving me to unpack, the adults finish talking in the lounge.

I'm happy to be on my own. It gives me a chance to look around my massive room the size of my lounge at home. Instead of darkness, there's light coming from every angle.

I feel like I'm standing in the middle of a big smile.

The walls, clean with lots of pictures of colourful flowers and people smiling, are so different from the walls I have at home. There's not one picture of God or Mary our mother and it sort've makes me panic a bit in case God sees and punishes me for it.

I won't tell Mother when I go back because she'll punish me if God doesn't.

Taking everything in, the horrible feeling I felt in my stomach on the way here melts inside me, feeling warm, fuzzy, and happy.

I'm not used to it.

How can this be all mine?

Sucking in the smells, smiling, there's no smell of smoke, piss, whisky or old mouldy clothes anywhere.

It feels weird but nice at the same time.

My double bed, the biggest bed I've ever seen in my life, is so clean that I worry I'll get it dirty with my dirty body, staring at the flowery duvet cover and pillowcases that match. The flowers, my favourite colour purple, are the same colour as on the two flowery cushions sitting on top.

How can a bed so big be just for me?

Running to it, landing on it, I'm lying on a cloud. There are no broken springs or damp blankets beneath me.

I could sleep forever.

The fluffy purple carpet looks soft as grass, taking my shoes and socks off feeling the soft spongy wool underneath my feet.

I'm walking through a field.

Worried I'll dirty the carpet with my feet, I quickly jump back on my bed and put my stiff, smelly, white socks back on.

I don't want to get into trouble on my first day.

I stink so much; I don't belong in a room like this.

I bet the family, especially the younger son, thinks that too.

The window right opposite my bed is open. The autumn breeze comes into play with my purple curtains, which have little tie backs. They look like they are dancing, which is how I'm feeling inside.

How do they know?

I've always dreamed of having a room like this.

Am I really here?

Dancing with the curtains, I don't know why, but I get up and jump and twirl like I'm a ballerina on stage. Twirling, twirling, twirling, I'm happier than I've ever been, imagining this is my home and Ava and John are my parents and I'm their daughter who they love more than anything in the world.

Twirling, twirling, suddenly I see something in the doorway and freeze.

I can't stop looking at him.

My heart is beating a hundred miles an hour.

Bradley stares at me.

His eyes frighten me.

Does he want to kill me?

I don't feel safe.

Pointing at me, he forms his hand into a gun and shoots me, looking at me with eyes that frighten me.

I don't like him.

Snarling, walking away, I slam my door breathing in and out quickly, watching through the keyhole to see if he is still there.

For just a tiny moment I let the fairytale take over me.

I can't let my guard down again.

The next few weeks are like a dream. Every day when I wake up my nose and taste buds are welcomed by the smell of freshly ground coffee, toast and if I'm lucky, pancakes. I hear Ava and John talking and bustling about and often hear music I've never heard before. They like their music which is something I've learned to love about them. Enrolled at another school, I miss Zoe wishing I could contact her. I know she'd flip if she could see me now. Well dressed, smelling nice and feeling loved, I love it here.

The calmness and kindness of my host parents is something I've never felt before.

They are the parents I've always dreamed of having, crying most nights because I know one day I'll be sent back to my monster mother again.

If I knew when I was going back I could prepare myself. They never let me know the exact day. Sometimes it's two weeks, other times it's eight weeks. I've been here for three weeks now. I'm sure they said I would be here for six but I can't remember if my brain is just telling me things.

I want it to be longer.

I want it to be forever.

I'm getting used to being clean and fed and I don't have any sticky hair full of nits or any clothes that smell of piss.

It won't last long.

I'll soon be back with my evil mother.

God won't be happy with me for saying that but I don't care. It's true. As much as I want to, I don't let myself think this could be forever. I know I'm just another child of many. The sadness I already feel about leaving is worse than knowing I'm going back. I'm sure the family only wants to give me something normal, something lovely to remember but do they or the social workers understand that the memory is sadder for me because I know I'll never get it back again.

I know I'll be sent back.

The following weekend Anton comes to stay. Waking up early, hearing music coming from his room, which is right next to mine, I'm glad he's next to me and not the other brother who, I'm glad, hasn't come to visit since the first day. Anton loves talking to me about music he listens to and I love to listen. He's taught me so much and introduced me to something called genres which I now know means different kinds of music.

Artists I've never heard of before have filled my heart with their words. Anton could easily have been a teacher. He's always happy to explain who people are and what artists were influenced by other artists when they were starting out.

I didn't even think about that sort of stuff when I started listening to music.

Hearing him talk gives me mind cuddles and I feel smart knowing a lot more about music. I'm happy about that. Wearing a different t-shirt every day with different people or groups I've never heard of, today he's wearing a t-shirt with just the letters, ACDC.

How strange.

Standing in his doorway, watching him carefully dust his record before placing it on the turntable, he's so tall that he has to bend to make sure there is no dust on the needle. He hasn't seen me yet, which I'm glad about because I love watching him. I love it when I hear the record crackle.

I've often thought he's like someone who waters a plant. I'm the plant but instead of giving me water, he's giving me knowledge about music.

I like that he sees how thirsty I am to learn.

Showing me different albums from his collection whenever he comes, he says I'm allowed to browse through them whenever he's not here.

He trusts me.

No one else trusts me like him.

What I especially love is hearing the crackle of the needle when it comes into contact with the record. It blows my mind that music actually comes out when you do that. My mother has a record player at home but I've never been allowed to touch it.

Today Anton's playing a record with the voice of an angel on it. Maybe God wants me to hear her. She's singing about dreams. Her voice is so different, so cool.

I wish I could sing like that.

Spotting me he smiles, inviting me in with a wave of his hand. He is so kind, showing me his album of the moment, *Rumours* by *Fleetwood Mac...*

Chapter Eleven

Rubbing the rough skin on my wrist and arms, I wonder what Anton is doing now and what he looks like? Has he added to his extensive record collection and if so, what with? I wonder if we met up, would we like the same music? I owe him so much for showing me such compassion and kindness all those years ago. I've often thought about visiting him to let him know that was the best six weeks of my life, but I always chicken out in case I see Bradley again. He'd made my life a living hell when I'd stolen the heirloom egg off the top of the cupboard and shattered it into a million pieces. The house had stunk for a week and Ava had cried every night. I felt so bad for doing that. Anton hadn't told me off or even made me feel like I'd done anything wrong.

He understood I didn't mean it.

It would be so lovely to see him again.

Placing my record on the turntable with the same care he used to use, I listen for the familiar crackle before 'Dreams' starts to play, singing along as Samantha starts meowing at me. The doorbell ringing interrupts me, having to place the cover on top of my player. Humming, hurrying to open the door, my usual postman smiles up at me singing along.

Incredibly small with goofy-looking glasses that make his eyes look like Mr Magoo, his front teeth protrude and the usual tiny bead of sweat on his forehead dribbles down the side of his face. I know he has a little crush, but he has a crush on all the girls who are nice to him.

He doesn't like Lola though.

He's said he senses something dark about her.

She's told me she thinks he's dodgy but none of the other girls feels threatened by him, me included.

In fact, we all think he is very sweet.

"Hey, Scott."

Looking anywhere but my eyes, he asks a question.

"Had any dreams about me lately? Ha-ha. Love this song, Jesse."

Gyrating and singing to the music, I'm a little uncomfortable watching him, signing for the parcel, cringing at the amount of words he's getting wrong. He can't dance either.

Laughing, adding a few moves of my own just to make him feel better, I'm dying inside.

"Looks like someone's got the hots for you, eh?"

A package with hearts all over it has my stomach churning with excitement. Surely not?

"Wow. I wonder who it's from? How exciting. I never get parcels. Thank you, Scott."

"Hope whoever it is knows what a lucky guy he is. I've got a few days off so see you when I get back, Jesse. Don't do anything I wouldn't do."

Blowing him a kiss, quickly shutting the door, and running to the kitchen, I open the drawer with the scissors and start to cut the parcel open.

"Who could it be from?"

Feeling sick, I can't stop shaking.

"Meow."

"Not now, baby. I have a parcel. *Me*. How exciting. Aren't you happy for me?"

Opening the box and lifting out another box with the words, 'open me' on it, a note and one perfect red rose is inside, the smell so intoxicating I think I might pass out.

Who is it from?

"Looking forward to seeing you next week, J."

Heart thumping out of my chest, my face is on fire, hoping, wishing it might be from Jayden? Does he know where I live? Bending down, fanning myself with my hand, I read the note again.

"Could it be him?"

Jumping, someone's banging on my door.

"Bloody hell."

A very sweaty Lola stands in front of me with two cups of coffee and two muffins.

What on earth is happening today?

Looking like she means business; she gives me the once over pushing me aside and letting herself in. Still sweaty from her aerobics, the familiar wooden scent of her perspiration fills the room. It's not like her to visit me here, this being her place of work, so whatever it is must be important.

Screwing her nose up at the fresh lavender I have on the kitchen table, she sits, making herself comfortable. Samantha snarls, hissing from the doorway obviously unhappy to see her.

"Fuck off, stupid cat, before I throw something at you."

"Leave Samantha alone. She's done nothing to you."

Removing her from the kitchen, Lola's face tells all. I don't know, but something tells me she's here to grill me on the conversation I had with Jayden last night.

I hope not.

She saw us talking for a while and snatched the napkin with Jayden's phone number off me before she stormed out. Maybe she's come to give it to me now.

God knows.

The buzz of receiving a flower for the very first time now well and truly spoiled by her, she'd better hurry up and tell me what she wants.

Tongue over her top lip, making a sucking noise with her bottom lip, she's definitely got something to say. As if I've read her mind, she looks me straight in the eyes.

"I'm not happy about last night, Jesse. I saw you talking to the new barman for a long time and he gave *you* his number. You? And put a heart in *your* drink. Why? I still don't get it. What the fuck was he talking to you about?"

I don't know whether to tell her the truth or just lie remembering what happened with Jim. Eyes narrowed, waiting for an answer, her arms, folded over each other, and tongue frantically licking her top lip backwards and forwards, I've never seen her so worked up about anything this much before.

Praying she believes me; I hope my face doesn't betray me.

"He was asking about you, actually, whether you had a boyfriend and how long I'd known you? I really think he wants to ask you out. He said you were the most beautiful thing he'd ever seen. The heart was supposed to be for you, he must've got it wrong. He told me to give you his number, but you didn't give me a chance to explain anything because you stormed out."

I don't think she believes me. Eyes bolting towards the package on the table, she picks up the card reading it, taking in every word. Killing me with slitted eyes, I know what's coming.

"What the fuck is this? Who the fuck is J? It's him, isn't it? You're fucking lying to me. Liar."

"Don't throw it, please."

It's too late.

Landing across the room, crashing against the wall, my rose's petals spread all over the floor running to pick them up, quickly remembering my chance meeting with Jim saying it's from him; that

I'd given him my address the night before. Accepting my story, backing down, she says she saw us together so knows I'm not lying.

Thank God she hasn't clicked that I would never have given Jim my address, not giving it to him the first time we'd tried to go out, why would I have given it to him now?

"I've already had boring Jim so you can have him. You'll find out for yourself how dull he is in bed."

Staring me out, like she knows something I don't, I stare back wanting more than anything to know what she is thinking.

"I know you're lying; you bitch. Don't ask me why, but I do. What the fuck are you up to? You of all people should know by now that I always get what I want. For all you know I might've already been underneath and on top of the new barman. Eh? What did you say his name was? How do you know I haven't already got there first? Eh?"

"Fuck off, Lola. I told you what he wanted. If you don't believe me then you don't believe me, nothing I can do. I'm not hiding anything. You've already destroyed the only rose I've ever got in my life so why don't you just get the fuck out and leave me to clean it up."

"Now, now, don't be like that. You know he isn't suited to you. You know he wouldn't look at you over me so don't go getting all excited that he would. I'll definitely get to the bottom of things. Who the fuck is he anyway? Where the fuck has this guy come from?"

Part Two

Patricia, James, and Jayden Rodgers

Sometimes you pray for a miracle hoping beyond all hope that some light will come into your world to brighten it up and make it worth living. I believe that's what my mother prayed for the day I was born. She prayed for a miracle. Little did she know what was in store. Little did anyone know. Be very careful what you wish for...

Chapter Twelve
Patricia

"You either get better or you get bitter. It's simple."

— *Josh Shipp*

February the 8th 1969

I t's a boy!
   Is it real? Am I actually a mum?
   I've waited so long, endured endless heartache, and protected my bump through so much, I think I might be hallucinating or making things up in my mind.
   Is my baby here?
   Is he finally here?

In a small hospital north of Wellington, laying on my back, looking into his pint-sized face, tears of joy run down both cheeks.
   Is this beautiful baby really mine?
   Holding him to my cheek so I can see his little face, I peer into it,

listening to his new-born gurgling noises, inhaling his smell, already a lioness ready to protect my cub from anything.

So perfect, his little nose, mouth, eyes, dark-black hair glued to his head are already imprinted on my brain.

How can anything be so perfect?

My lips whispering ever so softly over his soft spongy cheek, he is already the love of my life.

"I can't believe you're here, you're real. I've waited for you so long, my darling. I'll keep you safe. No-one will ever hurt you. You'll never have to suffer. I'll make sure your father never touches you. It'll just be you and me. I promise. I love you more than God loves you."

Wheeling him away to an incubator, my heart bursts with love, remembering the day the specialist had told me it was impossible...

... Calling me into his office with a face that already prepared me for the worst, he confirmed that my chances of ever having children was near to impossible stating my acute endometriosis was the cause. He added salt to my wound by saying it would take more than a miracle and an intervention from God for me to conceive. He was 99% certain I'd never have children of my own naturally.

"The best thing you can do is to go away, relax and never think about it again."

I wouldn't believe it. My whole life I'd dreamed of having children, so I had to hold onto the one percent chance he'd given me.

Leaving the office in tears and driving straight to the local liquor store, I bought a litre bottle of Jack Daniel's and drove home.

I don't remember much after that...

... Thirty-one weeks later, here I am, a twenty-two-year-old girl from the Kapiti Coast proving the specialist and everyone else wrong.

God had helped me carry him for this long, but He hadn't been able to protect me from the monster I live with who'd tried his best to destroy the only chance I had of becoming a mother. He'd beaten the shit out of me every given chance until my body couldn't take it anymore.

One emergency caesarean later, here he is, my miracle boy.

Hours later, holding him skin to skin, feeling his beautiful soft flesh on mine, inhaling his smell, the scent is already ingrained in my brain.

Squirming in my arms, my lips touch his tiny cheek, lifting his teeny-weeny hand in-between my thumb and forefinger, placing it to my mouth, the love I feel for him is immeasurable. Nothing could've prepared me to love this much.

I'd given in to all my husband's needs and wants to keep my baby safe, now that he is finally here, I know if I need to, I will kill to keep him out of harm's way.

Naming him Jayden, meaning 'thankful' in Hebrew, I'd always loved the name after hearing my mother tell me a friend of hers named her child that. I was only little, but the memory is so vivid. I'd never heard of the name before and thought it quite exotic so knew it would be the name I would choose for my first son.

Every day for a month Jayden gains strength and grows, soon able to hold him to my chest to feed him from a bottle.

Refusing my breast milk too many times, turning his little cheek to the side, it breaks my heart he does not want to feed from my breast. The nurses, seeing my distress, comfort me saying it is very normal for premature babies to do that. Accepting I will never have the bonding of breastfeeding, reluctantly I start feeding him from a bottle at the same time feeling my own milk drying up.

My one and only chance to nourish him from my body well and truly gone, I make up for it by holding him skin to skin while I give him his bottle.

At least I will have that.

I can't complain. Never in a million years did I dream this would happen. Never in a million years did I ever think I would be a mother.

Placing him on my lap, watching his beautiful face as he brings up his wind, tracing my finger over his nose, down his cheek, over his tiny head, his little mouth curls up into a smile.

My heart melts.

Lifting him carefully over my shoulder, gently rubbing his back, humming Mr Sandman in his ear, his fragility scares me. How on earth am I going to protect him from my husband? He beats me near enough every week.

Will he leave me alone when we arrive home?

How will I ever sleep knowing this gift I'm holding is at risk of being hurt?

What have I done?

Growing closer, loving him more than life itself, devoting everything I have to him, I vow nothing will ever come between us.

He will be mine forever.

The doctors and nurses say they've never witnessed such devotion from a mother to their child before calling him 'the miracle boy.'

Asking where his father is, I make excuse after excuse for his absence, secretly pleased he hasn't appeared. I want Jayden all to myself and have no intention of sharing him with anyone, especially his drunk father. The only person who visits me in the hospital is my sister who is delighted to see me happy.

She knows how volatile things are at home, but doesn't mention anything.

"You make sure to let me know if you ever need anything. Now that you have a little one it's very different. The love you feel for him now only gets stronger. Mum would've loved him, and dad. Such a shame they never got to meet our children. Keep him safe, Patricia. Guard him with your life. I'll visit again tomorrow."

Watching her leave, I know what she says is true. I won't see much of her once I am back home.

I miss her, wishing it was different.

I wish everyone would get on.

The day finally arrives for me to go home. Jayden, now weighing a respectable six pounds is wheeled out to reception by one of the nursing team with me clutching him for dear life. Expecting my husband to be overjoyed to see us, he's the exact opposite.

Refusing to come inside, James Nathan Rodgers, stands outside in a dirty light-pink tank top emblazoned with a busty blonde bombshell and a man in speedos kissing each other. His long black shorts, steel capped boots, and his favourite, 'I love potatoes' cap glued to his head, his face is thunder, hand on hip, puffing a cigarette as he sneers at Jayden, not wanting it to be real.

He hadn't once ventured near the hospital to visit us; I know why. He never wanted children, ever.

It's his worst nightmare and my dream come true combined.

"Let's get this fucking thing over with, shall we? Make sure that thing don't puke in my car."

Tall, dark-olive skin, black short greasy hair, broad unshaven face, his eyes are blacker than his soul, looking at the baby like he is poison. A broken nose from too many fights down the pub bends severely to the left giving the impression he's a boxer. He isn't. His teeth, a long time ago straight and white, are stained from alcohol and nicotine abuse, making his face less handsome than usual. Even so, he's still the looker seeing women stare at him on the odd nights we've gone out. It's probably his solid frame that they like. He has the physique of a rugby player which gives everyone the impression he's protective. Little do they know how wrong that is.

I know.

I fell for it too.

Chapter Thirteen
James Nathan Rodgers

I want that thing to die. I don't want it. I remember seeing my parents near enough kill each other before my father turned on me for a bit of fun. Why would I want to bring another human into the world for them to hurt? I decided from as early as five years old that I never wanted kids.

I never wanted that responsibility. I don't know or care how to love.

The thing squirming in her arms is a nuisance, another mouth to feed. I told her when we met that I never wanted any kids.

She'd tricked me.

Why the bitch is smiling and holding it to her chest like she's done me the biggest favour in the world by giving birth to it is something I'll make sure she pays for later. I warned her not to have any children, and watched her take her pill every night just for that reason.

How has this happened?

The night she came back from the hospital in tears, I had to calm her down so she could explain what the specialist had said. He told her having a baby would be impossible. That there would be zero chance of her ever conceiving.

Music to my ears.

The best day of my life.

I'd even let her off a beating thinking she'd already had a shit enough day. Instead we got on the source and had one hell of a party. She drowned her sorrows and I celebrated my good luck in finding someone who could never have the things I hated so much. The bitch duped me, told me she didn't even need to bother with taking the pill, that the specialist told her it wasn't needed anymore.

I believed her.

A month later, she's pregnant. I tried to kill it inside her, gave her a beating from hell, but she wouldn't let me near her stomach, had protected it with a force so strong, I'd sort've respected her.

I should've killed it when I had the chance. I hoped it might die when she suddenly went into early labour. Hell I'd even dropped her off waiting for the good news.

It survived.

The worst day of my life.

I'll make sure she suffers and so will the thing she contrived to be born into the world.

I hate them both.

Not offering her help getting into the car, instead I busy myself with lighting a cigarette and turning on my tape especially chosen for her. 'Back Off Bitch' booms from my speakers as all the nurses watch me pull out of the hospital car park, shaking their heads. Giving them the bird, not even checking to see if either of the fuckers in the back are strapped in, half an hour later we pull up fast outside the house.

"Welcome home, cunts."

Chapter Fourteen
Jayden

"Childhood should be carefree, playing in the sun;
not living a nightmare in the darkness of the soul."

— *David Pelzer*

April 6th 1975—age six

"You fucking bitch. I'll kill you, and when I'm finished, I'll kill him too."

Crash. Stomp. Bang.

Stop hurting Mummy.

Hiding in my wardrobe quiet as a mouse, I don't want Daddy to find me, or kill Mummy or kill me, too.

Mummy's running away from him. I think she's in my room.

"Baby? Baby where are you? It's Mummy. Baby, quick. We're going for a nice walk in the woods. We're going to play hide and seek with Daddy. It'll be fun."

I don't want to come out, I might give myself away and if

Mummy can't find me then maybe Daddy won't, too. If I move and he finds us, then we might die.

Inside my tummy there's a bomb that's going to blow up my heart, so I sneak out because if I don't, then Mummy might be alone.

"Stop crying, Mummy, I help you."

"Shhh, baby. Don't say a word."

Ouch. Mummy's hurting my lips with her hand and it's making me wobble.

Pushing me to a window, looking over her shoulder a lot, I think it's because Daddy's still shouting.

"I'll fucking find you; you bitch. Where are you?"

Jumping out the window, saying she'll catch me, I don't think she can because her face has black marks all around her eyes and mouth from where Daddy hurted her, and she looks like a skeleton at Halloween, like she's dead.

I don't want Mummy to die, jumping to her because she might need me if something bad might happen.

Running, running, running.

I don't like it dark. Mummy knows I don't like it dark but says I have to keep running and looking behind to see if Daddy is coming too.

I don't want Daddy to come too.

She's too fast and pulling my arm hard. I think she wants to pull my arm off and now I'm cold too.

"Mummy, stop running, I'm tired. Wahhhhh."

"Shhh, baby. I'll find somewhere safe for us to hide. Don't worry, it's a good game."

Stopping fast, Mummy puts her hand over my mouth and nose.

Ouch, it hurting.

The air won't go in. I don't want Mummy to kill me too, scratching her hands with my fingernails, but her hands have glue on them.

Thump, thump, thump. My head sounds like music.

"Baby, don't make a sound. Nothing. Wait until Daddy goes past. Promise Mummy? If he finds us he'll kill us. Promise Mummy."

I don't like dark, or cold, or Daddy, so I stop my eyes from blinking in case Daddy hears my eyelashes moving.

I try to stop myself going toilet, but I can't.

Mummy is angry.

"We can't go back to the house to change you. Why didn't you just wait! Now you'll have to sleep in your wet pyjamas."

Cold, I don't want sleep in my wet pyjamas or on leaves. The animals are scary and spiders making my face tickle. I don't want to sleep because animals might kill us too.

"I want go home, Mummy. It's too scary out here. I'm cold."

Making us creep like tigers to house, Daddy's waiting and calls us cats.

"Well, well, well, look what the cat dragged in."

I hate Daddy's scary eyes.

Hiding behind Mummy to stop seeing them, she never stops his eyes looking at me. She never stops my ears hearing his angry voice or his angry fists from hurting me. I don't look at Daddy, or speak anything to him because he doesn't speak nice things to me.

"Get your fucking feet off the fucking table."
"Who the fuck told you to fucking look at me?"
"Fucking eat your food."
"I never wanted you. Told her to get rid of you."
"You better do as your told, boy or I'll fucking kill you in your sleep."
"Get the fuck out of my sight."
"Get me a fucking beer."
"I'll fucking kill you both, you good for nothing pieces of shit."

Fuck, fuck, fuck, fuck, fuck.

Daddy says naughty words all the time. He says he hates me for being born and wishes me dead.

I hate him back.

I go sleep with one eye open, but how can I sleep with only one eye shut? Mummy must be magic if she can do that. I can't, but I won't tell her because she might get angry.

Tonight, Daddy's drinking his Jack Daniel's, beer, and gin again and smoking cigarettes and weed. He's too drunk to shout so is asleep on chair. Mummy says to relax and sleep, but I can't.

He might wake and hurt us.

When I sleep, a scary dream of a monster comes inside my head. The monster wants me to kill myself and my daddy. It happens all the time. It always there, clapping, happy. It, the monster, looks the same as me, but it scarier than even my father. I try not to dream of the monster, but I can't stop it from coming into my brain.

Mummy sleeps in same bed as me because Daddy might wake up and hurt me. I love it when Mummy's arms are my blanket. It breathes and I can feel its heart.

She has knife under pillow. I think it's to kill Daddy, but I didn't tell her I knew.

Some nights, when Daddy loses game at cards, or spends all money at the bookies or drugs, he comes home and drags Mummy out room like a rag doll and hurts her so much, I think he killed her.

I love her so much. I don't want him to hurt her.

I hate him hurting Mummy because I born.

She tells me I her miracle baby sent from God, but Daddy says God a cunt.

I put on my secret cape to stop Daddy's words hurting me.

"Why didn't you die at birth?"
"I should've killed you when I had the chance, you little prick."
"Don't even look at me or I'll kill you."
"Don't cry you little bastard or I'll give you something to cry about."
"You faggot. Crying like a girl, now are we? Man up, you little cunt."

If I died, like my Daddy wanted, then my Mummy would be safe and he wouldn't hurt her. I think there is monster inside him telling him what to do.

"You little bastard. Where are you? I'll fucking kill you. I told her never to have you. I wanted you dead, you little bastard."

Hiding under bed or corner of wardrobe when he yells, I put my hands over my ears to help me rock and block out Mummy's screams, but it never works, so I jump out window and hide in woods the same as I hided with Mummy. When I don't jump out window fast, Daddy finds me in one of my hiding places.

I don't know how he knows about my hiding places.

After he hurts Mummy, he makes me look at her – on the floor – with lots of blood. Then he yells and starts hurting me.

His eyes look like big black holes in the sky.

His eyes make me cry and go toilet because they are scary.

"Ha. Crying like a girl again. Boo hoo. You're not worth going to prison for, you little prick."

Mummy looks after me after Daddy hits me. She always cries and tells me she's sorry.

"I'm so sorry, my darling. I try to keep you safe from him but he's too strong. One day I'll get you out of this hell. I promise. Mummy will take care of you. Mummy loves you more than God loves you."

I think Mummy lies to me because she never stops Daddy. When she tells me lies I get a feeling, like fire that spreads from my feet to my brain, and I want to shake my body and scream.

But I can't and all the feelings stay inside me.

I don't believe her anymore. I don't know who God is and why He loves me more than she does?

I think I know why Daddy hates Mummy, because I hate her too, now.

I only six, which is only small. Mummy has told me not to lie because even a little lie is a sin, so why does she lie to Daddy?

If she lies then Daddy hurts us more.

I think she likes it when Daddy hurts her because today she took me to where he works and begged for money in front of lots of people.

That means he will hurt her when he gets home, and me.

I think she plays just a game. They both like to play game because it happens a lot. Daddy hurts us and then goes away four or five days. Then he comes home and cries and cries to Mummy.

"I'm sorry for hurting you, baby. You know I don't want to do it, but something happens and I can't stop it. You know I love you. It won't happen again. Please forgive me. I love you."

He looks really sad, even crying, so I stop hating him for a tiny second.

I start to watch closely when he hurts Mummy. Instead of hiding in wardrobe, I sneak out like a little mouse and watch through a tiny hole in sitting room door. Mummy cries and cries and Daddy listens only after a little while to stop.

I like to see Mummy cry and flop around like a ragdoll.

When I watch, I feel butterflies playing in my tummy and I wait for my Mummy's face to blood up.

I like the smell. I don't want it to stop and wait to see if he kills her. I wait and wait and wait and feel tingles inside my tummy.

I think Daddy knows I'm watching because he looks straight to the door I hiding behind and smiles.

He's never smiled to me before.

Mummy sounds like a dog crying when it's broken leg. I don't feel sorry for her like I would dog.

I hate her. I hate her and Daddy.

Chapter Fifteen

April the 20th 1975. The beginning of it all

S mack. Bang. Scream.

"You fucking bitch. You've tricked me again. You're pregnant. I told you never to have another baby. Never. You fucking bitch."

"I'm not pregnant. I'm not pregnant. Why would I be pregnant? We don't even have sex. What the fuck are you talking about? Leave me alone. Leave me alone. Arghhh!"

"Stop Daddy! Stop!"

I think Daddy's going to kill Mummy because her screams are different to normal but I can't leave the wardrobe because he might kill me too.

I want to see if he kills her.

Instead I put my hands over my ears and rock and rock.

Bang. Scream.

I think he might kill me, jumping out of wardrobe, opening bedroom window, and jumping onto foot marks from the other times Mummy has jumped. Running, looking behind to see if Daddy's running after me, in the woods my foot bangs something hard, falling over on the mud.

Leaves and mud and blood are on my leg, but I don't see anywhere hurt.

That's when I see a black and grey cat lying on its side with tongue hanging out and scary eyes, not blinking, not moving anything.

Tippy toeing softly, like a slippery snake towards it, the flies sound like planes in the sky, trying to zap them away with my hands, but it not working.

Up close, it's smiling and has teeth which covered with flies and little white bugs that crawling in and out of its mouth. Picking one up, it tickles my skin.

Silly bug.

That must be why cats smiling.

Because the bugs make it tickle.

There's some blood, the same as what's on my leg on its leg, too.

What's happened to poor kitty?

Finding a stick, using it to turn the dead kitty over, it's heavy, like one of the pots in my kitchen but a bit more heavier. Seeing the hole on the cat's leg, I put in my finger and the insides come out and look like jelly.

Running back to the house as fast as light, hiding behind window, checking to see if any noise from Daddy, when I don't hear any, I jump back through window landing on floor with a big thump.

I'm glad I practised playing blind man's bluff at school.

Waiting, trying to hear Mummy or Daddy talking, I can't move. My eyes are like Superman looking through door. There's no yelling or smell of cigarettes, so I unstick my feet and tippy toe exactly ten steps to my bed, finding Mummy's knife under pillow.

I think I should check to see if Mummy is dead, so I softly open door and go look for her, finding her in sitting room, on floor, not moving.

I think she's dead.

Walking right up to her, I see her close and she isn't dead because her chest is breathing in and out.

I'm glad I didn't miss seeing Daddy kill her.

She should be dead because both her eyes are puffy. They look funny, like a fish, poking one with my finger, feeling it squishy, like it's got lots of water inside. I like it. Her chin looks black and sometimes blue, and her mouth is open, making lots of funny noises. The blood dribbles out of her mouth and she lies in puddle, on the wooden floor next to her arms above her head. She looks like she's dancing on floor.

Her light brown hair is red, but I've seen it red before.

Kicking her hard in the side, her body is like jelly, all floppy and heavy and wobbly.

I hate her.

I hate Daddy more.

The rumbling, like a thousand cats all purring at the same time, comes through the walls. He's asleep, tippy toeing to his bedroom, seeing him lying on top of the bed, still holding onto bottle of Jack Daniel's. Daddy's face and fist are same colour as Mummy's hair. He not look scary at all. The monster inside must be asleep, too.

The cat?

Running to the kitchen I get a cloth and plastic bag and put knife inside. Wiping cat's blood off my leg with cloth, it goes in the bag with the knife, opening back door, running as fast as I can back to cat, which is still lying on ground, smiling, waiting for me.

It's heavy, dragging it behind a bush by its tail. Only the man in the moon can see me.

Next to dead kitty, the butterflies in my tummy make me feel excited, talking to dead kitty, telling it I'm going to be very careful.

I don't know why?

My knife by its tummy, cutting its skin, it doesn't move. The skin is hard, like elephant skin. Cutting more into it, it's pink inside and spongy, like how my tongue feels. Something gooey spills out.

More blood.

Blood starts coming out fast over its fur and me when I cut its neck and it smells bad. Its blood is everywhere on me, I don't want to stop.

I'm happy, excited.

I don't want the feeling to stop, cutting its eye and scooping it out, looking at it, looking through it like a mirror. Sniffing, smelling the blood on my hand, it's different smell to Mummy's blood. It smells like my silver money, but a little sweeter.

Running down my hand, the blood tickles to the end of my fingers and then it goes to the ground and makes it red.

I love the dead cat. It's my friend.

Carefully putting the knife back in the bag, I don't want to leave kitty, but I have to because I'll get into trouble if I take it back to the house. Insects are already eating its insides; I can't stop watching.

Keeping hold of eye in my hand, thinking of places I can hide it, no one is ever going to take it off me.

Ever.

Chapter Sixteen
Patricia

My heart yearns for another baby. They are so much easier, more loving, and babies need you, rely on you for everything.

They love you the way you need to be loved.

Jayden's detachment from me is like a knife to my heart, having caught him sometimes looking at me like the monster we live with.

I need someone to love me.

I need to have a purpose in life for something.

James might soften if I give him a little girl. The beatings might stop once I'm with child again. Deep down I know how he'll react, but I hope that he might have mellowed, mustering all the strength I have, bravely broaching the subject one night.

"Are you fucking joking, you stupid bitch?" *Slap.* "Another child?" *Slap.* "I didn't want the first fucking one so what makes you think I'll want another one?" *Whack.* "You fucking lunatic. You dare trick me into having another kid I'll fucking kill you all with my own two hands, you hear?"

Slap, kick, slap. Thud.

Giving up on the idea, I know he'll follow through on his threat if

I don't. We aren't even having sex having shifted into Jayden's room months ago.

I would've given myself to him one more time though if it had meant having a playmate for Jayden.

He is my life now so I need to make sure nothing happens to me or he will suffer. I can't have that, won't have it.

Over the next few months, laying low, James sells possession after possession to fund his addictions; all I can do is watch.

One night, pushed to my limit, enough is enough.

Knock, knock, knock, knock, knock.

Bang.

Peering through a slit in the wood, trying to see who is outside, it's 6.30pm. Who could it be? No one comes to visit.

"Who's there? What do you want?"

"I'm here for your car."

"What the hell are you talking about? Why do you want my car?"

"I won the fucking car in a game of cards. Now hand over the keys."

"I haven't been told to give you my car, now piss off and leave me alone."

"Mummy tell the lady to fuck off, why does she want our car?"

"Shhh, never mind darling, Mummy just needs some time to talk to the lady. Go back and finish your drawing. It's bed time soon so hurry up."

Looking up at the most colossal person I've ever seen, she is in fact a he and stands, sweating, sneering down at me with his fiery, tangerine, unruly hair frizzing all around his face. His big bushy beard, moustache, and eyebrows the same colour as his hair, drip with sweat; his angry bloodshot eyes stare straight into my face, curling up his mouth ready for the next verbal assault. Towering over me, his massive body is sweating under the strain of his weight, the grubby Rolling Stones t-shirt he's wearing showing every bulge. Dark purple shorts far too small for him cling like a second skin as he jiggles from foot to foot in his tiny sandals, black from where his feet and toes have smudged the plastic with dirt.

He is far from happy.

"Wow that's a real nice kid you have there, lady. Look, it's just taken me nearly an hour to walk here. I'm not leaving without my car, which I won fair and square in a game of cards. I'm real sorry to come here like this, but you need to speak to Jimmy about it, not me. I just want what's mine. I'm real glad I didn't agree to take the kid. Jimmy told me what a little prick he was."

"What? Jimmy? Take the kid? Are you telling me the truth?"

I know he's not lying.

No one could or would have made that up.

I don't wait to find out.

Begging him to wait and drop us off at the train station, he reluctantly agrees as I quickly pack a small suitcase and a few toys for Jayden, grabbing the few thousand dollars I've managed to save over many years, from the inside of my favourite hedgehog garden ornaments. Hiding the money in my bag, snatching Jayden and his drawing up from the floor, I tell him to wait with the bags as I quickly scour James' drawers for any money. Underneath a pair of his socks I find a box of matches with the name *The Orchard*. Why does he have these? In very faint writing I see a name that has been written and scribbled out. The name starts with A. Who is it? What does it mean? Grabbing them, securing them in my bag, I quickly check we have everything and take Jayden to the waiting car, jumping in with the stranger I've just met.

What am I going to do?

Where am I going?

I don't care. Anywhere is safer than here.

Thanking the man, whose name I find out is Bill, he reassures me that he wouldn't have agreed to taking Jayden but there were plenty of others who were more than happy to.

"Look lady, your boy is safe so don't think about it anymore."

Waving, watching him and our car drive away, I make sure

Jayden is glued to my chest not believing how close I came to losing him. Blood boiling, shaking, crying into his soft hair, if James was here, I'd kill him.

"Mummy, why are you crying?"

"It's nothing darling. Mummy's just sad the car has gone, that's all."

I know exactly what I have to do.

"We're going to see someone special. Someone you haven't seen for a very long time."

The train station, busy tonight, is full of commuters on their way home or going into town. Jayden's hand, fastened to mine like a second skin, is slippery with sweat trying to escape from my clutch. I can't risk anything happening to him, quickly dragging him to the ticket office and purchasing the tickets needed. Clinging to my leg, crying to be picked up, he's restless, grumpy, and tired. I haven't got the strength to hold him.

Seeing my train leaves from platform six at 19.32, I grab the suit-case and bags, leading Jayden by the wrist to find two seats on the next available train to the only people I think will help us.

Chapter Seventeen

I n a luxurious spacious house just outside the suburb of Porirua, about twenty-one kilometres from Wellington, lives my sister, her husband and son. Not exactly sure how long it's been since I've seen or talked to them, I fell out with them at a family gathering years before defending James's drunken behaviour yet again.

"Get that fucking kid's arse off the fucking table. That's where we eat for fuck's sake. Have some control over your fucking kids. Jayden, get your fucking shoes, we're leaving these assholes to it. Patricia. Help him find his fucking shoes."

Sitting on the train, my mind full of memories of that day, I hope my sister will have forgotten about it, or at least forgiven me for my rotten taste in men. Watching Jayden, who's thankfully fallen asleep on the two seats opposite, covering him with my thick jumper, I'm so happy to see him so peaceful, beautiful, and calm. A yellow mark fading on the side of his head makes the guilt I feel double, brushing the hair from his face, stroking his forehead as he sleeps. At least now we will only have each other to worry about. At least now we are both safe from James's violent hands.

Leaving him to sleep, sitting back and reaching into my bag for some gum, the drawing I grabbed in my rush to get us out of the house sits on top. Carefully unfolding it, trying to make as little noise as possible, I'm excited to see what Jayden has drawn.

Staring in shock, shaking my head from side to side, the stress of the last hour and a half must have me hallucinating.

This can't be right.

It's so detailed, so unbelievably shocking. It must be a joke, something he's seen and copied. A child his age can't know of things this evil? Each part has been drawn to utter precision. There is so much I recognise.

But there is some I don't.

The cats.

What is he doing to the cats? It can't be his picture. Not my son. Not my baby's.

Sleeping like an angel opposite me, the drawing I'm staring at is the complete opposite of anyone angelic. Has his father's darkness passed to him? Is he the same? No one can see this, checking to see if anyone behind me has seen it, scrunching it up and putting it back in my bag to burn as soon as I can.

No-one but me can see it, ever.

Gazing blankly out of the window, the noise of the engine is loud as it combines with my thoughts, nervously twiddling my thumbs, looking around the carriage to see who is on the train with me. Two young men to my left curse and swear in their ripped, turned-up blue jeans and t-shirts that have images of the Sex Pistols on them. Black heavy eye make-up and piercings through their septum remind me of two bulls, nearly laughing out loud giving myself away. Spiked, painted red hair will be sure to put anyone off approaching them to find a seat; I'm wishing I hadn't sat so close. Their dirty, black Dr Marten lace-up boots rest on the seats in front of them as they talk loudly to each other. I'm surprised they can hear what each other is saying by the loudness of the music coming from their earphones, both completely oblivious to the sleeping child next to them. Their look is conflicting with the smell radiating from them. Almost spicy, the aroma of the lovely sandalwood oil one of them has on reminds me of my youth and how much I used to love burning incense of the same smell. Smiling at the juxtaposition of it, the distraction from my thoughts is welcomed.

Fuck, seeming to be the only word they know, doesn't bother me, but a few others turn to look.

Both young men and their greasy complexions full of pussy spots are making me feel a little queasy. One with a cigarette over his right ear, keeps fiddling with it, as his beady eyes scan the passengers provoking them into a confrontation. He looks my way darting my eyes to an older woman ahead who's talking quietly to the person beside her. Looking back disapprovingly at the noise coming from the back; her face contorts and hands fly about looking in the young men's direction. Thankfully they are in conversation and don't see her.

The rails of the train hit many bumps as the carriage jiggles from side to side keeping Jayden asleep with its steady rhythm. 'God save the Queen' plays from one of the boys' headphones, thinking it must be incredibly loud in his ears if I can hear it from where I am. Fearful to ask him to turn it down, I'm unsure how he'll react, busying myself with peering out the window, resting my head on the glass. I don't need any more confrontations today.

Trees and sea whizz by as the sky changes from blue to red and yellow, making diamonds dance on the water as the sun sets.

It is so beautiful.

The loud humming of the aircon unit making conditions bearable in the hot carriage is almost deafening, Jayden making me jump as he suddenly kicks the thick jumper covering him off while a baby a few seats up screams. It may want food or a drink, the crinkling of a bag being opened hinting that its demands are being met. Whilst its mother tries to distract it from crying, one of the young men beside me moans to his friend.

"We have to walk all the way from the fucking station."

Clunk, clunk, clunk.

The next carriage's clunking signals it possibly needs oiling.

Ding, ding.

The train stops.

The doors open.

"This is Johnsonville," announces the robotic woman on the sound system.

The two men make their way to the door, relieved the noise from their headphones will no longer disturb me. More people jump on, the rails whirr to a start and the train sets off once again.

The faint smell of marijuana has me looking around wondering where it's coming from, seeing a young girl with red eyes who has just entered, sitting in one of the vacant seats left by the young men.

The smell reminds me of James.

I wonder what he's doing. If he's already looking for us.

Only about fifteen minutes away, I will have to wake Jayden soon but I'll leave him to dream a little longer.

Pulling into Porirua Station, suddenly I can't breathe thinking about the phone call I'll have to make.

What will I do if she says no?

Where will I go?

I haven't been to Porirua in such a long time, just the increased number of people is encouraging me to turn around. Feeling faint, dizzy, trying to distract myself by waking Jayden, he's having none of it.

"Fuck off."

Crying, kicking, and punching me, it's a struggle to pick up his heavy body, but I finally lift him and fasten him securely to my left hip at the same time grabbing my suitcase and handbag, which I fling over my right shoulder. A man offers to help, quickly backing away, flinching.

I don't want any man near me or my son.

My suitcase and Jayden are heavy, finding the strength I need to walk towards a line of people waiting to use the phone. The same man who offered to help looks at me like I'm crazy.

Maybe I am.

Jayden cries.

"I need the toilet."

"In a minute."

Crying on my shoulder, he's so heavy. My legs feel like jelly. How has he got so big?

Placing him on the ground next to me, walking forward to the phone booth, I lift the receiver.

Chapter Eighteen

B rrring, brrring, brrring.
"Hello this is Ava."

She sounds the same.

Chirpy and a wee bit high pitched, this is the first time in forever I've heard her and my heart feels like it might pop out of my chest and run away.

Forehead sweating, throat like gravel, I don't know if I can even speak.

Should I just hang up?

My head wants to explode and Jayden isn't making it any easier banging his little hand against my hip.

"Mummy I'm thirsty, where's my fucking juice?"

"Hello, who's there?"

"Jayden, stop."

Silence.

No one speaks.

Jayden screams, punching my hip while I grip the phone to my ear speaking very slowly, holding onto him with my other free hand.

"Ava? Are you there? Ava? It's me... Patricia. I'm at P-P-Porirua Station. I've left him."

Silence.

Has she heard me?

My heart is banging against my ribs.

It's so loud.

The noise of the station dulls around me. Jayden screams by my side. My hand hurts from gripping his wrist, bending down, screaming into his face, begging him to stop.

"Stop it, Jayden. Be good for Mummy. Please?"

Suddenly I hear her voice.

"Patricia? Porirua? Left him? What do you mean? Is this really you, Patricia?"

Crying into the receiver, anxious that my desperate pleas of help have been heard by others around me, I whisper.

"I can't live with him anymore, Ava. Please, can we just come stay with you for a few weeks until I can sort a place out? I don't have anywhere else to go. Please? Ava?"

Silence.

Seconds feel like minutes.

Anticipation.

What is she going to say?

Jayden cries.

"Shhh."

I'm going to faint. My throat is dry.

Waiting. Waiting. Waiting.

"Wahhhhh."

A man yells at me impatiently from behind.

"Hurry up, lady."

Ava answers.

"I'm not happy about this, Patricia. What the hell do you expect me to do? Ringing up like this out of the blue. You haven't spoken to me in years. *Years*. Lots of things are happening here. It's not a good time for you to just appear out of nowhere, but I can't bloody leave you sitting at the train station, can I? What am I going to tell John? Let me go and speak to him and I'll pick you up in about thirty minutes. Why didn't you get off at Paekakariki? It's much closer. You can stay for two weeks. Max. After that you have to find somewhere else. Understand?

"Thank you so much, sis. I owe you huge. You won't even know we're there. I've missed you so much. I'll leave in two weeks, I promise."

"Promise?"

"I promise. Cross my heart and hope to die."

"I'll be there as soon as possible."

Returning the phone, moving my shoulders up and down, trying to relieve some of the tension of the call, they are stiff and heavy, like two rocks either side of my head. Rolling my neck from side to side, gently rubbing my left shoulder with my left hand, my right hand tries to control the weight struggling to get out of my grip. He's not helping, bending down to eye level, trying to catch his other hand, which seems to have a mind of its own.

Slap.

Whacking me across the face, I throw him to the ground screaming. Resting my forehead on the wall next to the phone, my heart tries to regain its normal rhythm as my hands protect myself from the little legs and arms flinging themselves at me, punching and kicking. Grabbing them in midstream, holding both his arms and looking down into his angry face, he spits.

"Stop it. You have to be a good boy now. Your aunty said yes. She's coming now."

"Hurry up, lady, I want to use the phone."

Not interested in what I'm telling him, Jayden continues to punch, kick and spit.

"I want to go home. I'm hungry."

Apologising to the man behind before I drag our belongings, and my screaming child, to a spare bench, I look around for the exit noticing the place hasn't changed at all from the last time I was here.

The island platform has the same waiting room with restrooms either side taking me back to the many times my family took the train to the Kapiti Coast to visit my grandparents. I would stand on a similar platform at the other end waiting for them to come pick us up. That must be why Ava had chosen to live there.

Remembering the day she had boldly asked our parents to send me back, I can't help but giggle.

"Why did you have to have another child? Why did you have to have a girl? I wanted a brother. Can you send her back?"

Laughing, my parents had explained there was just no way they could send me back and that she was stuck with me, her little sister forever. She had to find a way of liking me.

I wonder if she still feels the same.

"Mummy, what's funny? I need a piss."

Shaking my memories away, Jayden punches me in the side, grabbing his arms before they hurt me anymore.

"Stop it. You hear? Don't hurt Mummy or I'll hurt you."

Embarrassed, catching disapproving looks from passers-by, I'm not sure whether they are for me or for my screaming child.

One old, short plump lady with white, tight, curly hair, a weathered face with moles that protrude from her forehead, chin, and cheek, boldly limps straight towards me with her walking stick. Close enough for me to see her tiny slits, her whole face grimaces like she is in pain, her thin wrinkled thin lip's part, almost spitting the words at me.

"That child needs a good slap."

Like a witch with a forced grin, her wild unfriendly eyes don't wait for me to respond, turning her round body and walking stick around and walking past a few people on a bench who clap as she passes nodding her head at them.

I can't help myself.

"What do you know? You ugly old bitch. Leave us alone, you hear?"

Grasping the suitcase, and Jayden, who is still screaming, I have to get away from them, rushing towards the entrance, him howling the whole way.

"I need a piss. Fucking stop, you bitch."

The same people on the bench sit shaking their heads back and forth, glaring at them as we pass. Would they have more compassion if they knew how I'd come to be at the train station? How I'd nearly lost the child they so openly disapprove of to who knows who tonight? Would they be so judgemental then?

Drawing a protective arm around Jayden, sneering at them, I don't care what they or anyone thinks.

"Come darling, let's find you a toilet."

Thank God I still have him. Thank God he is still able to punch and kick and scream. Only God knows what could've happened to him if any of those monsters' playing cards had come to claim him.

What would I have done if that had happened?

I wouldn't have been able to stop them.

I could've lost my baby forever.

Kneeling down, looking into his dark troubled eyes, there is so much guilt and anger for what he has put up with, not only today, but forever. Drawing him close, hugging him to me and picking him up so he can rest his weary head on my shoulder, I gently soothe him, protecting him from everyone's judging eyes. He is my baby after all and I still love him more than life itself.

What will Ava think? Will she look at him the same way these people are?

How will she look?

Will John be ok with having us stay?

How old is my nephew Anton now?

Realising just how much I've lost touch with them, I softly rock back and forth calming Jayden down, whispering in his ear.

"Are you ready for the toilet now, darling?"

Nodding to me, putting him down, taking his little hand in mine, I lead him to a toilet I've spotted ahead.

The tiny restroom is difficult to navigate, leaving the suitcase to the side while Jayden complains of the smell. I don't blame him. It's a cross between stale blood and rotting food, which is enough to make me want to turn around and leave. Catching sight of the bin full of sanitary towels and hypodermic needles, I pull Jayden away quickly guiding him into one of the two tiny cubicles, locking the door, listening to see if anyone comes in. The incessant dripping of one of the taps isn't helping.

"Wahhhhh it's dirty. I don't want to sit on it. It stinks."

"Just get on and then we can get out of here quickly. Hurry up."

"Wahhhhh."

Pulling down his track pants, standing him over the filthy bowl, he refuses to do anything, losing patience with him and myself. It's so claustrophobic. As he pees, my own bladder screams to be emptied, the dripping of the tap outside not making it easy for me to hold, quickly moving him out the way, squatting over the bowl while he pulls up his pants. I daren't sit for fear of catching anything, quickly squeezing everything out as someone comes in the door. I'm sure she's crying, escorting Jayden to the small dripping hand basin, side-stepping a young pregnant girl holding her stomach.

"Are you alright love?"

"Yeah I'm fine lady. Just having a bad day, that's all."

"Anything I can do to help?"

"Yeah, if you've got $5 spare, I'd love to buy some food?"

Grabbing my purse, guessing she isn't any more than fifteen, sixteen, her stomach bulges out of her flimsy green t-shirt and filthy blue dungarees. Shivering, even though it's warm outside, she's rubbing her stick thin arms while her black, grimy, puffy feet which look to be retaining a lot of fluid, rock back and forth in her open toe sandals. Pretty, her freckled drawn face is weather worn showing lines that shouldn't be on someone so young; tired, sad, green almond eyes plead for warmth. Skin, full of greasy spots, her medium-length blonde hair, tied in plaits is just as oily. Resembling a frightened, half-starved bird, I can't help but feel sorry for the frail, tiny thing holding up a sizeable bump protruding from her stomach.

Opening my purse, handing her $100, I wish I could give her more.

"Go get yourself a night in a hostel and some food. Have a long soak in a nice warm bubble bath and rest up. Perhaps go to a shop and buy yourself some clothes that fit? A nice warm coat too. Here, take another $50."

"Wow lady, thanks. I mean it. You're like an angel or something? I won't forget you."

Hugging her, seeing the bruising on the side of her head and marks around her wrist from where she has obviously been grabbed, I remember back to when I myself was pregnant and had to protect myself from violent hands. Guessing she is on the streets; I wonder where she lives.

How she's surviving?

Has she gotten into the state she's in by force or consent?

Not wanting to embarrass her, asking how old she is, the pungent odour coming from her mouth as she answers is hard to ignore.

"I'm sixteen. I know, don't tell me, pretty stupid or what? It wasn't planned. You don't know who you're gonna 'bump' into on the streets.

Pointing to her protruding stomach, she attempts to make a joke.

"I'm not keeping it, don't worry. The guy told me he loved me, would take care of me, but he ran as fast as his feet would take him when I told him about the baby. I thought he loved me. He told me he was leaving his wife and good for nothing kid and was gonna come get me. Haven't seen him in months. Men? Looks like you got a good one, a nice boy too. I'm gonna find someone nice to take this one. It's gonna have a good life, different from mine. I'm Gail by the way, pleased to meet your acquaintance, angel lady. Thank you. I won't forget you."

In the blink of an eye she vanishes into thin air leaving me wondering if the exchange has been real or something I've imagined. Running out of the toilet, looking around to see if she is still near, there is no sign of her or her bump anywhere.

"Wahhhhh. Mummy where's my fucking food? I'm hungry."

Walking back into the toilet, quickly grabbing Jayden, who is now distraught, I hug him close.

"I'm sorry, darling, I forgot you were even there. It's not like you to be so quiet."

Perhaps he'd sensed the importance of the exchange between myself and Gail and had had the good sense for once to keep quiet?

Miracles happened.

I thought I had it hard. I couldn't imagine being so young, pregnant and on the streets. That poor girl. Whoever had walked away from her was an asshole and should be ashamed of themselves. At least James had stuck around. At least he hadn't walked away from me when I'd become pregnant and had accepted Jayden, eventually. That son of a bitch, the pig who'd caused Gail to become pregnant and then walked away. He'd surely be going straight to hell.

Praying she will keep safe; I can't help but hope to see her again someday?

"Ava."

Collecting our belongings, running towards the exit like we're in a race, Jayden's still screaming for food, punching me. Ignoring the disapproving looks of passers-by, quickly glancing up at the huge clock in the terminal, no wonder he's playing up. It's past eight o'clock, he must be starving. Nerves keeping my own appetite at bay, I spot a little truck selling food just outside the entrance ordering chicken and chips for Jayden and a bottle of water for myself. Sitting down on a bench close to the car park, Jayden scoffs his food like he hasn't eaten for weeks.

Pulling on a jumper, my thoughts are now completely focused on Ava, scanning the car park at every car entering.

Is she near?

So many cars come and go, I don't have a clue what I'm looking for. Jayden will need bed by the time we get to hers which will give us time to talk.

Watching him lick his fingers one by one, I pray to God he won't play up and will allow us to catch up.

Sneaking a chip from his box of food, glancing up to the sky above, the dark silhouettes of birds hovering hoping to pinch a scrap of food is gorgeous behind the dusky sky. Jayden belches loudly, startling not only me, but himself too, laughing, throwing his scraps to the birds, watching as they glide down and surround the area where we sit. Squawking, fighting each other for food, Jayden gulps his drink like a plant in a drought. I had no idea how thirsty my little man was, spitting onto a tissue, wiping his face clean.

A red Volvo 4-door pulls into the station.

I know it's her.

Holding my breath, watching as she opens the car door, one tiny leg emerges, then two, then a whole body. Locking her door, looking around, she is smaller than I remember and now wears glasses; her short, cropped, brown hair makes her look frumpier. She's put on a bit of weight, noticeable through her plain trousers and clumpy pale-pink jumper but it suits her. Spotting me, smiling, waving, running to give us a big kiss and hug, we embrace, crying with happiness to see each other after so long.

"Let me see you. You've lost so much weight, Patricia, you're a bag of bones. And look at you, Jayden, you've grown so much darling."

"Wahhhhh, who's this, Mummy? I don't fucking know her. Get off, you bitch. Can we go home now?"

"Let's get you back to mine. John is making the double room up for you now and we can put him straight to bed. He's probably exhausted from the journey, the darling."

Driving back to Ava's, chatting about nothing in particular, she suddenly asks what has happened and I have to explain we can't go back, looking back to Jayden who's busying himself by looking out the window.

I know he's listening.

We're out of danger for now, but for how long?

147

Both he and I know we could be dragged back to the monster we've left at any time. He could be waiting for us already at Patricia's.

Jayden sits rubbing his head from his latest beating.

"She's lying. My dad said she's a good for nothing bitch and said he'll kill us. My mummy has a knife."

Snatching a sweet from my bag, giving it to him, his drawing sits on top, burying it deep to the bottom. Punching and kicking me as hard as he can, I can't control him.

"Fuck off, you stupid bitch. I want to go home."

There is so much confusion and terror in his eyes.

Trying my best to hold his wrists, I understand his torment.

"Stop it, Jayden. Here, take the sweet before I change my mind."

Taking it, staring out of the window, rocking back and forth in his seat, the guilt for what his little life has been like up till now is huge. He's probably panicking about the next time we will have to face his father, deathly afraid of the beating we'll both get if he finds us. James won't hold back.

Ava's sympathetic eyes say nothing for the rest of the journey.

Driving for another thirty minutes, we pass Paekakariki, Paraparaumu and Raumati before turning into a tree-lined Kanuka Close. Arriving at Ava's magnificent double-storey mansion, John and Anton have heard the car and come outside to greet us. The porch lights click on seeing John who is still tall and thin with hair that seems less sparse and glasses that have changed from rectangular to round. They make his eyes look even tinier. Still, he is smiling even though it is a nervous looking one. I imagine he is a little shocked by the sudden reunion. Waving at me, coming down to give me a big hug, Anton, who I've been told is now twelve, follows him.

The image of both his mother and father, he is all smiles as his gangly legs nervously approach, hugging me, peeling Jayden, who is crying, off my leg and asking if he wants to go inside and meet their pet cat Tiddles.

Tears miraculously stopping at the mention of their cat, for just a tiny second, I'm worried for Tiddles safety remembering the drawing in my bag. His excitement and delight quickly making me brush it off, I'm ashamed how I could even think of it.

Following John, who has grabbed the suitcase and bags, we walk up the stairs to our room.

"I'll put the kettle on and make us a nice cup of tea," Ava shouts from the kitchen.

Leading me to the last room on the left, John leaves me to unpack and freshen myself up.

"I hope it's ok for you, Patricia? It's really lovely to see you both."

Patting my shoulder, making his way downstairs, I step inside, overcome by the size of the guest room and how much space there is.

Underneath a ceiling that reaches to the moon sits a super king size bed, walking to it, touching my nose to the pillows, inhaling the fresh, clean smell, instantly taken back to the last time I was here. A cross between lavender and lemongrass, a wave of nostalgia flows over me remembering that is Ava's favourite scent. A perfect white duvet covered in beautiful red poppies with pillowcases to match, have two fluffy red cushions that sit side by side on top. Walking around the bed, turning on one of the flower-shaped lamps that sit on each of the small wooden side tables, the bulb inside is dim, bringing a calmness to the room. Parking myself on the side of the bed, I can actually breathe without having to worry if anyone will walk through the door drunk and angry. My mind and body have been conditioned for so long to react at a minute's notice, the feeling of calm is making me feel a little anxious, all of a sudden overcome with the what if's.

What if this isn't real?

What if James is on his way?

What if, what if, what if.

Feeling like I've run a marathon, I rest my head between my legs begging my mind and body to let it rest, just this once. Underneath my feet a fluffy beige rectangular floor mat rests on top of old dark wooden floorboards, counting the stray strands, continuing to breathe. To my left, a huge set of dark woven wooden drawers sits underneath a window and on top of them sits a glorious spider plant happily showing off its long green and white leaves which point to a little plate full of potpourri, the scent mixing with the smell of the fabric softener on the sheets.

Clean, crisp and dust free, my sister has always been house proud.

I wish I was the same.

Standing, facing the wall next to the door, are pictures from long ago. I hadn't noticed them when I walked into the room because it'd been dark, but with the help of the light, I see faces of people I love winking, smiling, and laughing at me. Surprised how much Jayden looks like me at the same age, I'd always thought he was his father's double.

Pictures of Anton and John at different stages of their lives hang off the walls. It's so lovely to see happy faces of people who love each other. Ava and John's wedding shot is particularly beautiful, remembering the day with happiness. My parents sit either side of us, the love in their eyes beyond compare.

Touching the picture, suddenly my heart hurts, kissing my fingers, touching their faces.

A rocking chair I've noticed sitting beside the window looks the same as the one my mother used to have.

Is it hers?

Walking a few steps to it, placing myself amongst the red and yellow velvet flowers and leaves, I carefully lay my hands on the dark curved walnut handles, closing my eyes, transporting back to being a little girl sitting on my mother's knee. Rocking, I'm with her, smelling Lily of the Valley, her favourite scent.

Has Ava sprayed it or has the smell somehow managed to stay?

I would do anything to have my mother near.

Not visiting her or my father's grave in years, the heartache of losing her was too much. Always Mummy's girl, losing her so suddenly and then my father soon after, sure he wasn't able to live without the love of his life, had sent me off the rails; my life had changed in the blink of an eye.

I met the monster.

I'd been planning to leave this world the very same day I found out I was pregnant. I'm sure my mother stopped me, knew what was living inside me would help keep me alive.

That's what I like to believe.

Suddenly I can't breathe. My parents, the furthest people from my mind for so long, are stirring up feelings I've ignored, suddenly making me feel like I'm floating around in a room overloaded with memories I can't stop. Gasping, hand to heart, it is breaking all over again, rocking backwards and forwards frantically in the chair, breathing, peering out the window, steadying myself on the window ledge. I can't handle it. Especially after the day I've had.

Something scurries across the path outside distracting me. A perfect white cat runs from Anton and Jayden who are following it. Thank God he is getting along with his cousin, the playful noises a welcome surprise after such an emotional day.

Pulling myself up from the chair, feeling a little calmer, I trace my fingers around the intricate carving of the wood at the top. It is so beautiful, like my mother, sure I can feel her energy close.

"I love you, Mum."

Not expecting a trip down memory lane, or to have added to the emotions of the day, I'm sure my mum has been looking over me for years, certain about one thing. She'll be happy I'm safe with Ava.

Unzipping my suitcase, searching for Jayden's pyjamas, laying them out on the bed, I'm not looking forward to the tantrum he's going to have when I have to detach him from the cat. His little body should be weary after so much today, quickly placing our clothes in the drawers lined with scented paper that smells of roses, a scent also connected to our mum. Not usually emotional, that little gesture from my sister means so much.

Entering the ensuite bathroom with our toothbrushes, Ava really has made sure I need nothing, even leaving out towels with trains on them especially for Jayden. A few bath toys probably from when Anton was young sit along the bath.

Why is she being so good to me?

I don't deserve it.

She's taken us in at such short notice, how will I ever repay her?

Placing our toothbrushes in the glass jar next to the tap, peering at myself through the mirror, I look so worn down, so drawn, the lines on my face so pronounced, the harshness of the light making me look like a hag. Not a hint of makeup on, I can't remember the last time I wore it. James hadn't allowed me to wear it for years, afraid other men would look at me; find me sexy.

I used to be so sexy, so desirable.

No man would look at me now, let alone find me sexy.

Except him.

The monster I live with.

His face stares back at me, laughing through the glass.

How have I let it get so bad?

Ava must think I'm pathetic, not even able to look after myself let alone my child. The lightness I felt only five minutes before now weighed down with feelings of shame, hopelessness, and failure, especially where Jayden is concerned, I hear him squeal downstairs reminding me I should be with him. Breathing in deeply, shutting my door and making my way downstairs to where Ava and John are waiting for me at the kitchen table, it doesn't take long for them to cut to the chase.

"What's really going on, Patricia? What has James done? Why can't you go back? I don't think you told me the whole story in the car. Remember that was when Jayden started up. Is he always that angry at you? He's very much like his father in that respect, isn't he? I can't say I'm not surprised. I just wonder why it's taken you so bloody long to leave?"

Head bulging from all the questions, it could burst like a bomb; my brain, already at maximum capacity, would probably pop if someone pricked my head with a needle. I've tried my best not to take Ava's comments personally and tried not to cry, but my chin won't stop trembling.

"I'm so sorry. It's really bad now, at home. I had to get out. The gambling, drinking, drugs, and temper I could deal with. You heard Jayden in the car? I sleep with a knife under my pillow just in case he comes home drunk and follows through on his threats of killing us."

John and Ava's eyes meet, expecting they're both thinking the same thing. John's clearly not happy, eyes flickering from side to side, mouth pursed tight, like he's holding something in his mouth. He says nothing.

"Tonight, something just snapped. I've had enough. I'm not allowed to have any friends. I'm not allowed to work. He doesn't let me out of the house except to take Jayden to school or go shopping, only for a certain amount of time, but even then, I have to make sure I have receipts for everything. If I don't have the exact money he hits me. All of that I can deal with, even the beatings, but the bastard used Jayden as a prize in a game of cards tonight. My son. His son. I was this close to losing my boy."

Squinting, using my thumb and forefinger to show just how close I came, I hear my own words out loud and something inside me snaps.

"Some man nearly won him in a game of cards. I couldn't take the chance he wasn't telling me the truth. And yes, Jayden is angry all the time because he has to be ready to run, protect himself if his father decides to pick on him after he's finished with me. He's terrified for his life. If he ever turns out like his no-good son of a bitch father I don't know what I'll do? What would you have done if you were in my position? I didn't know what to do."

Hard to breathe in-between the tears running down my face, they're choking me and my heart and head won't stop beating, like they're in a race. Dizzy, sweating, breathless, the anxiety of nearly losing Jayden catches up, choking as Ava quickly shoves a brown paper bag under my nose telling me to breathe in and out of it. Slowly rubbing my back with the softest of hands, I hear her, but all I see is Jayden, trapped in some strange man's car, screaming for me from the back window, and I can't do anything but watch, and scream myself.

"Breathe in, breathe out, breathe in, breathe out, breathe in, breathe out. Slowly. Now focus on the small black and white tiles. Count them, Patricia. How many can you see? Breathe in, breathe out. That's a good girl."

Slowly, breathing returning to normal, the dizziness subsides and the panic is over for the time being, but Ava still pats my back, asking.

"Now tell me about the man. Slowly and calmly."

John, who has poured me a glass of water, hands it to me with a box of tissues. Angry with what I'd just said, his slim face is a shade of purple and looks like a volcano that's about to explode. Staring straight ahead at Ava, who's signalling to him to say nothing, she gestures for him to sit down. Nostrils flared, like a bull ready to charge, I swear I can see steam coming out while he pours himself a glass of red wine and gulps it back in one.

Blowing my nose, wiping my eyes, sipping my water, I need something stronger.

"You don't have another glass of that wine do you, John? I could really do with one."

Pouring me a glass, handing it to me, patting my back and squeezing my shoulder tight, I automatically flinch, freezing on the spot, apologising straight away, gulping the wine in one.

"A huge ginger-haired man turned up at my door earlier this evening telling me to give him the keys to my car. Said he'd won it in a game of cards. I told him to fuck off, I wasn't giving him the keys to anything, but he'd just stood there, getting angrier and angrier until I handed them over. He was massive, the biggest man I've ever seen in my life. I didn't know what to do. I couldn't say no. James has sold everything. We're lucky to have a bed to sleep in. The television, radio, furniture, Jayden's bike, pictures on the wall. They've all gone. It's so hard, I didn't know where else to go. When the man told me James gave him a choice, the car or Jayden, I didn't hang around to see if it was true. I begged him to give us a lift to the station. We were just lucky he won because he said there were other men who'd already agreed to take the boy. The bastard. What if I'd lost him? What if the bastard had given away my baby?"

She has no time to answer.

All of us hear a commotion coming from the sitting room.

"Come here, you fucking bastard."

Tiddles hisses angrily.

"Don't grab her tail, she doesn't like that. Stop."

"Don't come near me, I'll fucking kill you.

Slap. Meow.

Wobbling back and forth, entering the kitchen with a huge red mark across his face, Anton looks stunned, in shock, holding Tiddles tight.

"I only suggested he not grab her tail. Tried to help him play with her nicely."

Bursting into tears, I can't take anymore, shaking at what has just happened to Anton, filling up my wine and gulping it back as tiny black holes stare at me from the door daring me to go near him.

"I want to go home. I fucking hate it here. Why are we here?"

Hugging me, John jumps from his chair to tend to Anton, who is still standing, hand to face cuddling Tiddles who jumps from his arms up onto the work surface. Placing a bag of peas on Anton's face, John picks up Tiddles to comfort her. His angry voice echoes throughout the kitchen.

"You can't go back there, Patricia. He's too dangerous. I'll bloody kill him. I've seen the bruise on the side of the boy's head."

Pointing to the door he yells.

"Was that him? Did he hurt him? Did he cause that bruise? No wonder the boy is like he is. You can't blame him? If he goes back, he'll end up like him, or be given away to perverts who'll kill him, or worse, rape him for the rest of his life. Do you want that?"

I've never seen John so angry, and by the looks of it, neither has Ava, who's staring, open-mouthed, at his red angry face. Sitting back on his chair, his energy levels decrease as Tiddles rubs herself against his arm, probably sensing his mood, meowing, jumping in his lap and allowing him to stroke her beautiful white fur. From the door Jayden flings himself at her, desperate to have her. John grabs Tiddles with one hand and Jayden with the other, making sure his cat is safe.

"No Jayden. Leave her alone."

Frothing at the mouth to get to her, Jayden's like someone possessed, eyes fixated on the thing he wants. Mouth snarling like a tiger hunting its prey, we all watch, waiting for him to calm.

Ashamed, knowing John is right and that Jayden is a carbon copy of his father, I've just chosen to ignore it, pretend it hasn't existed. I've deliberately distracted myself from the obvious inherited traits by whatever was going on in my life. The last thing I want to admit is that Jayden is more like James than myself, having prayed to everything I could that he might've changed over time. It's obvious my prayers have been ignored.

Suddenly remembering the picture he drew; they might understand why he's like he is. Give him some leeway.

It's not the right time.

It's been enough for them for one night. Tomorrow will be a better day to do it. For now, it's enough just to be safe.

Jumping from John's lap, Tiddle's runs out the door, away from her tormentor who screams and kicks.

It's time to put him to bed.

The phone rings.

"It's him, I know it is. Don't tell him we're here, please. He'll come and get us. We can't go back."

Gesturing for me to be quiet, Ava picks up the phone, relieved to hear it's just one of their friends asking something about school. Holding her gaze, waiting for the conversation to end, I gulp more wine as John listens from where he is, still holding Jayden who has calmed enough for him to now let him go. Returning the phone, reassuring me that even if James calls, she will not be telling him we're here and that she and John will keep us safe, Ava sees me trembling and tells me to take Jayden to bed. He must be worrying whether his father will turn up.

"Don't worry, darling. It's bedtime."

Nodding, a different boy walks, head slumped, obediently following me, crying, and yawning with exhaustion. It's been quite a day for him with all the travelling and change. I have to remind myself; he is still only six. Little eyes that have witnessed far too much for someone his age fight hard to stay awake. I will make it up to him, I have to make it up to him, make it right for us both. Undressing, changing him into his favourite Thomas the Tank pyjamas, I don't bother with brushing his teeth, laying his little body in the bed. Ten minutes later, he's asleep, twitching as he dreams, hoping his thoughts are happy. Watching him for another five minutes, making sure he's covered, I kiss the top of his head and leave, keeping the door open a little bit if he should waken.

Passing Anton's room, knocking, asking to go in, I hear music, knocking again, this time a little louder so he can hear. Music pausing, he opens his door looking at me with swollen eyes; a little bright red mark across his face, like a beacon, reminding me how violent Jayden has been to him.

I feel so ashamed.

"Are you ok, Anton? I feel so bad for what happened before. I'm sorry you had to put up with that tonight, and I'm sorry Jayden hurt you when all you were doing was being nice to him. Please, can you find it in your heart to forgive him? He's been through so much today; I think all the change and exhaustion has just caught up with him tonight. I'll make sure he apologises to you tomorrow. I promise."

Moving forwards and giving him a hug, I'm happy he allows me to embrace him and isn't too cross. Letting go, he looks at me puzzled.

"It's ok, Auntie Pat. I'm sure Jayden didn't mean it. I'm sure it will all be ok tomorrow."

"Thank you, Anton. That means a lot to me."

Looking around his room, there are lots of posters on the walls of his favourite music artists, and a record player in the corner has a shelf full of records underneath it where Steely Dan sits on top. Walking over to the player, picking up the sleeve, I'm amazed he even knows who they are.

"Wow, Anton. I'm impressed. Do you like Steely Dan? A little old for you isn't it? Nice record player. Was it John's?"

Seeing his eyes light up at the mention of music, he tells me it was his dad's, and all the records too and that he's making his way through them one by one. Just like his dad, he loves his music, a real chip off the old block.

"I'll look forward to coming in to have a browse through them over the next few weeks. If you'll let me?"

Bending his head to the left, his smile is all I need to see.

"Of course, you don't even need to ask, Auntie Pat. Anytime."

I really hope he and Jayden will find some even ground for getting along. I hope Jayden will give his older cousin a chance.

Meeting Ava in the sitting room, she's already there.

Exhausted, the tension in my shoulders, head and body feel like lumps of lead with all the burdens and guilt I'm carrying, deliberately diverting the conversation away from what has just happened and instead asking Ava about how much both of our lives have changed. We talk about our childhood and how happy it was, mentioning the photos in my room and how they've brought back memories long forgotten. I ask her about the heirloom egg in the cabinet, amazed it is still intact, telling her she mustn't let Jayden anywhere near it. We talk about what will happen now I've finally left James and what the future holds for Jayden and I, realising just how much I've missed having someone to talk to, to be close to.

Minutes pass into hours and before I know, a bottle and a half of wine later, it's after twelve o'clock and time for bed. My shoulders feel a little less heavy as the effect of the alcohol successfully numbs my guilt. It's quite rare I feel this way, always having to be ready to flee if James becomes too violent.

It's wonderful to feel safe.

Weary, feeling fuzzy and warm, I hug Ava goodnight tiptoeing up the stairs, making sure not to make any noise. The more I try, the more noise I make, bumping into walls, nearly knocking over a plant standing just outside the study at the top of the stairs. Clumsily walking in my bedroom door and undressing on the way to the bed, I watch Jayden as he sleeps, seeing one of his little legs uncovered, both arms sprawled out like an angel above his head. Lips open wide, sleeping on his back breathing heavily, he's taking up a lot of the space, but I don't mind. It's the most relaxed I've seen him in a long time. One of his legs and an arm moves involuntarily as he sleeps, hoping more than anything that his dreams are happy.

Never having had a full night's uninterrupted sleep, we usually both sleep with one eye open, listening for clues or noises that signal we need to hide or run.

I'm so happy he is able to sleep soundly and deeply at last.

An owl hooting outside startles me.

Not used to hearing anything other than James's usual snoring, I stumble to the window and peek outside, covering my breasts with my hands as I watch with fuzzy eyes for the bird in the darkness. It's so still, so quiet, no noise, just me, the bird, and the trees, which are motionless, lit up by the fluorescent orb in the sky. Hooting again, I spot the owl in the tree watching something from a branch, its white plumage beautiful in the silhouette of the moon. I wonder what sort of owl it is. The only one I know is a Morepork.

Flying out of the tree, its magnificent wings move fast and my hazy eyes struggle to follow it, swooping to grab a rodent, clutching it in its sharp claws, making its way back to the branch to feast on its body. Tiddles appears sitting below the tree watching as the owl rips apart the dead animal with its beak. Her shiny white coat sparkles like a diamond in the moon's glow as she patiently waits for scraps to fall her way.

Eerily quiet, the non-noise is deafening, only hearing my heartbeat as I peer out at the dark world.

Finding my pyjamas on top of the rocking chair, I clumsily pull them on hearing movement behind. Turning in a panic, Jayden is sitting up, staring straight at me, watching, eyes wide open.

Is he awake?

Yawning, laying back down on the bed, closing his eyes, he sleeps again.

Tiptoeing to the side of the bed, leaning over him, checking to see if his eyes are closed, his body suddenly springs up again and his eyes look straight at me making me jump.

Screaming, he's terrified.

"Jayden, wake up. Mummy's here. I'm here darling."

Screaming, crying, arms thrashing about in panic, his eyes remain open like he is awake? I don't know what to do. Ava knocks.

"Is everything alright in there, Patricia?"

Running in, coming to my side to help, we each grab one arm trying to calm him, soothe him, tell him everything is alright, but he doesn't hear us, doesn't recognise our voices.

"Don't want to go. Don't let the man take me, Mummy. Leave me alone."

Staring at me, Ava starts crying, making me cry. Helpless, unable to control or soothe Jayden, he thrashes about in a panic, screaming, and just like that, his body flops, and the screaming stops. Letting go of his arms, watching as he turns on his side and goes back to sleep, we both stare at each other in shock.

"What was that, Patricia?"

"I don't know. He's never had anything like this before. I'll kill James. I feel so guilty. What have I done? What have I done to my baby?"

Hearing the owl outside, we turn towards the window listening to Tiddles meowing and hissing below.

"Get some rest, Patricia, he's ok now. Get into bed and cuddle him. The darling, he's been through so much. So have you. You both need to rest."

Closing the door, blowing me a kiss before she leaves, I snuggle up to Jayden, who is snoring. Closing my eyes, my mind won't relax, still a little hazy from the wine. I can't unsee James giving Jayden away.

So close to losing my precious boy, hugging him close, smelling him, making sure he is real, I thank God he is still here.

I will never forgive James.

Never.

Moving my hand back and forth over Jayden's little back, comforting him as he sleeps, eventually my hand stops of its own accord and somehow, I also fall asleep.

The following morning, awakening to the sun smiling through my window onto my bed, I reach for Jayden for a cuddle, the bed is empty.

Panicking, running from my room, down the stairs, screaming his name, Ava strolls out of the kitchen stopping my panic.

Holding him in her arms, he's eating a banana.

His father's eyes stare straight back at me.

It scares me.

I hate that their eyes are so alike.

Why couldn't he have had my eyes, my colour, my shape?

Glaring at me, he's not in any rush to leave Ava's arms, pulling her close for a hug, asking if she can take him outside to see Tiddles.

"Don't you want to go to Mummy first, darling?"

Looking straight at me, smiling, he almost spits the words.

"Fuck her."

Shrugging her shoulders, Ava looks confused.

The phone rings.

Waiting for it to ring off, frozen as the beep of the answerphone kicks in, I pray it won't be James.

Beep.

His voice roars through the kitchen.

Jayden screams.

161

"You fucking bitch. Bill told me what you done. Told me he dropped you at the train station and I knew you'd go and see your fucking ugly sister and her retardo husband. They're the only ones who'd have you. What the fuck are they gonna do? Save you? You got two weeks to get your asses back here before I come looking for you, you hear? You ain't nothing without me. Nothing. Who do you think you are? No-one will ever want you, you ugly bitch. No-one. You'll come running back. You ain't nothing without me. You and the thing ain't nothing, you pieces of piss. Get your fucking asses back here or else."

Jumping from Ava's arms screaming, Jayden's little legs scramble to the garden. Running after him, grabbing him by the scruff of the neck, hugging him tight to me, he is too strong, his arms and legs bashing me everywhere, hitting and kicking me hard.

"I fucking hate you. I hate you both."

Chapter Nineteen

Two months later John's been able to pull a few strings with friends at the council and help secure a place for us to live. A tiny two-bedroom, fully furnished flat in Miramar in the outer suburbs of Wellington is very close to the airport, which Jayden will love. James hasn't bothered trying to contact us again. I can only guess he rang to scare us and that he was more than happy to be rid of us.

Relieved he is out of our lives at last, we can all look forward to a bright new future and can finally let our guards down with no threat of anything happening.

Jayden's outbursts have lessened, but his nightmares about his father have increased. He wakes in a sweat dreaming he is being killed by his tormentor or being given away to strangers. His dreams are fractious, terrifying, and relentless, leaving him exhausted. Tucked away in his subconscious, the thoughts appear once his mind thinks everything is safe.

It will be something that will affect him his whole life.

Tiddles still hasn't warmed to him and avoids being anywhere near him. Anton, I know, senses something isn't quite right and watches, protecting his beautiful cat from his cousin's dangerous eyes. I know he's relieved to hear we'll be moving.

The night before we leave is all the reason he needs.

Not I, or anyone else could've predicted what was going to happen.

Ever...

... Holding a little going away party, Ava, John, and I sit around the table toasting to new beginnings. Reflecting back over the last two months, saying how happy we've been reconnecting, Ava's a little preoccupied calling Tiddles to be fed, shouting for Jayden and Anton to come for something to eat and that she wants to announce some exciting news.

"Tiddles, spp, spp, spp. That bloody stupid cat. Jayden, Anton, dinner."

Laying the food on the floor for Tiddles, she turns, grinning, looking at me like the cat that got the cream.

"We've finally been approved to foster. I haven't told you because it was all still being approved but, after two years of interviews and courses and counselling, we're finally here. They'd like to speak to you now if that's ok? I told them I had no idea where you were and then when you came back, they were delighted. Is that ok? They said we can start straight away. Our first foster child is coming next week."

Excited, hugging them both, they'll be fabulous foster parents. The way they've treated Jayden over the last few months is proof. Celebrating with another glass of champagne, I'm so glad things are looking up for all of us. It's been a hard two months, especially for Jayden, who seems to be turning a corner at last.

It all goes wrong in the split of a second.

Hiding behind the door, I see him telling him to come celebrate with us, but something's off.

He's smiling, but not in a good way.

I've seen that look before.

Carefully walking towards him, not sure if he's holding something, I try to coax him out.

"C-c-come show us, darling."

Walking into the middle of the kitchen, standing, grinning at me, Ava and John haven't seen him, still chatting, clinking glasses.

Right hand, covered in blood, holds up a drawing as blood drips down onto the floor. Left hand, raised above his head, holds a carving knife, also dripping in blood, jabbing the air, staring.

What has he done?

Possessed with something dark, he laughs, watching all of us.

Is this a dream?

Blood drains from my body.

Terrified.

Frozen.

Ava screams.

It's not a dream.

John stands numb, as do I, looking in horror at the picture he's holding. Why didn't I destroy it when I had the chance? Somehow my legs move slowly walking towards him, trying to grab the knife.

Snarling at me, ready to pounce. I don't know what to do, backing off.

Following the knife above his head as it jabs the air, I want to grab the picture, the knife, but I'm too far away.

"Where did you get those, darling? Have you been playing with some paint? Such a dirty boy, now I'll have to give you a bath. We can put all your favourite toys in. Come on, darling, give them to Mummy."

"No. Fuck off, you bitch. I'll kill you like in the picture. I'll kill you and Daddy. I hate you. I hate him. I hate it here."

Waving the picture, grinning like the devil, we all stare in disbelief at the gruesome scene he's drawn.

Standing over a headless corpse of a woman in bed, a boy holds up what looks to be her head with his right hand and a knife with his left. Cats lay everywhere. Behind the house are some dark woods, and beside them a house burns and the words arshole, bich, cunt, die, spew from the windows. A large wardrobe in the house is full of eyes and a boy sits smiling, holding up an eye. It is titled, 'Monsters'.

Staring in horror, looking at each other, not knowing what to do, Jayden holds the picture and dripping knife, looking straight at me, grinning.

How can a child of six have done this?

It can't be happening.

Shaking, terrified, panicking, Anton has snuck into the room unseen by Jayden.

Eyes wide with terror, we all watch him.

Sneaking in from behind the door, gesturing for us all to shhh, he slowly tiptoes towards Jayden who hasn't noticed where our eyes have moved. Jabbing the air with the knife, we don't even dare blink as Anton gets nearer. One false move could be fatal.

Right behind Jayden, grabbing the knife from his hand, Anton throws it to John as I run forward and grab the picture. Wrestling Jayden to the floor, Anton sits on his little body securing him to the floor.

"You evil little bastard. I'll fucking kill you."

Squirming to be released, Jayden laughs.

Ava screams.

"Anton. Stop. He doesn't know what he's doing."

"Oh yes he does. The evil little fucker."

Pulling Jayden from the floor, securing both arms behind his back, Anton looks at us with fear so intense, we can't ignore it.

"Wait till you see what he's done. Tell me he hasn't got the devil in him?"

Marching Jayden up the stairs, still holding both his arms behind his back, we all follow, not saying a word, except for Jayden who's screaming like something evil is trapped in his body trying to escape from it. Continuing to resist his cousin's grasp, he kicks and tries to bite him from behind like a wild animal.

This can't be my child.

It has to be an imposter.

A devil inside him.

Walking in silence past pictures that have been marked with blood, the wood on the stairs has similar streaks and the carpet is stained with red and black goo, following all the way to Anton's room. Staring into a scene straight out of a horror film, we stand, open-mouthed, not believing it's real. Jayden can't have done this. It has to be a bad dream. Surely, he isn't capable of evil to this degree?

Squirming in his cousin's arms, desperate to get inside the room, his eyes have taken on a strangeness I can't explain. It's as though someone else I don't know is controlling his mind.

Whoever it is, is not six years old.

A six-year-old couldn't know of such atrocities.

Could they?

Jayden's clothes and body, covered in the same red foul-smelling blood, drip with remnants of paint onto the wood below. The smell, a cross between blood and paint thinner, is making our eyes water, covering our noses to stop from being sick.

Inside Anton's room it is carnage. Every record, cover, and sleeve are broken, scratched, and cut up. Each poster has been slashed; blood oozing from the necks of each person on it. Blood and black paint on the ceiling above the bed drip like acid rain onto what is left of the covers, and duck feathers from the insides of his pillow and duvet lay in a clump in the middle of the room, mixed with the same black paint.

On top of everything lies Tiddles, their beloved cat.

Still perfectly white, except where her throat had been slashed, her tongue hangs out of her mouth as dozens of flies' hover over her head landing on one lifeless eye which stares straight ahead at nothing.

Where is the other eye?

Managing to free one arm, Jayden retrieves something from his pocket and holds it up. Throwing Tiddle's eye into Anton's face, it bounces off, landing where Tiddles lays.

Ava screams.

Anton howls.

John stands numb.

Jayden smiles. The last thing I see is the floor as everything turns black.

We left that night.

Ava and John immediately put the house on the market.

I don't see my sister again until the vigil.

Chapter Twenty

"To ignore evil is to become an accomplice to it."

— *Martin Luther King*

W as he born evil? Was this God's way of punishing me for daring to ask for him when I knew my body couldn't, shouldn't have had a baby? Should I have just let James kill him in my belly?

Asking the same questions over and over, trying to make sense of what happened at my sister's, not wanting to believe that my only child, my baby, was capable of such cruelty, such hatred, such evil, why hadn't I seen it?

How had I been so blind to it all?

Was Jayden just a carbon copy of his evil good-for-nothing low-life father?

I don't think even he would've been capable of such evil.

Would he?

I'm not sure I know the answer.

. . .

Standing in the doorway of Jayden's room, head feeling like a gas cylinder stretched to its limit, if I were to put a flame to it now I'm sure it would explode and splash my thoughts all over the walls around me.

Watching his little chest rise and fall as he sleeps, he has the face of an angel without a care in the world, his tiny eyelids moving backwards and forwards falling deeper and deeper into a slumber.

What is he dreaming about tonight?

His night terrors have all but disappeared since we've been here, so it's not his father who visits his dreams.

Does another monster visit him?

One who helps him, encourages him to do the bad things he does?

Does that monster take up residence in his tiny brain, too?

Tonight, he's exhausted from his sports day at school, which is good for me and hopefully even better for him. Tonight, I am hoping his brain is too exhausted to dream.

"Just rest, little man, just rest."

His beautiful full lip's part and tiny bits of dribble fall from his mouth to his chin which his hand must sense because all of a sudden it wipes the dribble away and the spit, now on the back of his hand, transfers to his sheet. Moving, kicking off the covers, exposing his tanned legs, he must be hot.

He looks so beautiful in his sleep, no one would believe he'd be capable of hurting a fly let alone slaughtering an animal the way he'd done with poor Tiddles. The images of that night are permanently imprinted on my brain, the carnage too much for even me.

The sorrow he'd caused the whole family had been excruciating, torturous, especially as they'd been so loving and looked after us at a moment's notice.

Why had he done it?

What had that poor cat ever done to him?

The extreme hurt he'd caused. They didn't deserve it. No one did – except me.

The guilt eats me alive every day sitting like cancer in the pit of my stomach where it spreads to every part of my body until I can't move from the pain.

Why can't I just forget it?

Pretend it never happened?

Why can't I forget the look of pleasure on his face as he'd stood watching the family collapse in shock; smiling, like he'd done the best thing in the world.

He'd held the missing eye of the killed animal like it was a prize.

It terrified me.

I'll never forget it.

Ever.

Sometimes I think I conceived a monster and the devil had a hand in creating him and that God had tricked me.

What was I going to do with him?

Would he kill again and if so, should I abandon him, disown him now?

How could I?

He was still my son, my baby, half of me.

Leaving him to sleep, making my way to the lounge, physically rubbing my thoughts off the wall, questioning everything, blaming myself for it all, my ever-present glass of cheap red wine welcomes me, soothing any bad thoughts I have. I choose the cheapest because that's all I can afford, and I get more for my money. The vinegary taste isn't nice, but that comforts me in a way, knowing that I don't enjoy it. At least by not enjoying it I'm punishing myself in some way.

Lifting my feet up on the couch, tucking them under my bum, clutching my glass like my own prized possession, I stare at a photograph on the opposite wall of Jayden smiling, looking like any other little boy.

Praying almost every night to anything I can that he will miraculously change, I hope more than anything he'll suddenly wake up one morning an angel.

. . .

Two months pass and neighbours have started accusing him of touching their animals, adamant he's responsible for their pets disappearing. Prize goldfish have gone missing from a neighbour's pond and a fire above the corner shop no one can explain has nearly cost a young family their lives.

Has he added arson to his repertoire of sins?

In my gut I know he has.

I don't want to believe it, and will only believe it if I see it with my own two eyes.

Adamant to prove myself and my neighbours wrong, I don't know why, but one day I follow him unknowing that this will be the worst and best day of our lives.

Chapter Twenty-One

18th July 1975

Keeping a good distance behind, Jayden walks down the street, turns sharply left, winds around the back of where we live and creeps into a garage that is full of different pieces of furniture.

Permanently locked, it is only accessible by the person who owns it, which isn't me.

Keeping up with his little legs, I can tell he's up to no good by the way he keeps looking around to see if anyone is watching. My spying is nearly compromised at least twice, but he seems preoccupied with what he's doing, continuing to follow him, me creeping into the garage behind him via a side door that has been broken into.

How has he done this?

Surely, he is too little to know, too weak to break such a thick lock?

A thunderous humming from inside makes me jump. What is it? Inside, a tsunami of flies' thrashes towards me, black, buzzing, brutal. Swatting thousands of them away, they bang against my skull like a hammer having to push against them like a strong wind, letting my arms blindly lead the way.

Unable to cover my eyes, nose, and mouth from the onslaught, lowering myself to the ground, I crouch behind a chair watching as he makes a beeline for a huge double wardrobe. Opening the double doors, more flies escape as he looks around nervously and steps in.

Someone from outside is calling.

"Tobias, dinner time. Come on, old boy."

Roger, the old man who lives three doors down from us is looking for his cat. His cat? Moving closer to the wardrobe, panicking, gagging at the overpoweringly strong smell which is a cross between sulphur and very strong nail polish, I feel faint, covering my mouth and nose with my arm, my heart pounding, tiptoeing closer, begging my lungs and head not to give up.

Near enough to listen, I place my ear to the wardrobe trying to hear above the buzzing flies. Jayden's talking, laughing at something in there with him.

What is it?

Meowww, hiss.

Oh God.

A cat.

What is he doing?

Peering through a hole, holding my breath, swatting the flies away, seeing the old tabby, Mother of God what is he doing?

Watching in horror, Roger is still calling, getting nearer and nearer to the garage. I don't know what to do. Should I ask him for help?

"Tobias, spp, spp."

The cat, on its back, is hissing and scratching at Jayden who has his hand around its neck. Fighting to be released from his grasp, a knife is raised, seconds away from plunging it into its flesh.

"Tobias, dinner time."

Jayden, hearing Roger, turns, laughing as the knife hovers in the air inches away from the cat's eyes. I can't take any more.

Bang.

Smashing the doors open with both arms, thousands of flies escape from behind them into my face and eyes. Blindly grabbing for the knife above Jayden's head, screaming in agony as the tip of it slices into the top of my arm, he roars with rage, kicking, and screaming as Tobias scratches him before bolting for freedom. Jayden following the cat, I stop him, tripping him with my leg as I pull the knife from my arm and throw it to the garage floor. Hardly able to hear the sound of steel on concrete, the buzzing above my head is deafening.

Snatching hold of Jayden's legs, suddenly I'm super strong, tugging him towards me, screaming, bending down, shaking him violently by the shoulders. Close enough to see the floor, it looks to be moving, worried the smell has affected my brain.

The flies are everywhere.

It's too much.

"What do you think you're doing? What in god's name makes you do this? They're going to take you away. Do you understand? They will take you away, to another place to live. Away from me. To a stranger. Is that what you want?"

Laughing at me, I want to kill him. I want to retrieve the knife from the ground outside and end it all, but instead I grip him by the arms and yank him to his feet, inspecting my throbbing arm to check the cut isn't too deep. Looking up to a scene straight out of hell itself, my head feels like it's on a spring bobbing from him and his smile to the carnage around me as eyes of all different sizes stare blankly at me from everywhere. I'm in another horror movie, terrified, staring in disbelief at animals' heads that look on in different stages of decomposition. Some of them look to have been freshly killed, still dripping with blood, which falls to the moving floor. Cats' heads and one tiny dog stare at me with one wild eye, tongues hanging, covered in flies and maggots crawling in and out of different cavities. The smell is disgusting, nauseating, my stomach and head can't take it, vomiting as

I hold on to Jayden, wiping my mouth, swearing I can see the devil smiling back at me.

"What have you done?"

Dragging him back to the flat, passing Roger who is watching, stroking Tobias, Jayden bites my arm desperate to get to the cat again.

Conscious of my bleeding arm, I quickly swap sides, smiling as sweetly as I can, calmly waving hello as Jayden rips at my hand to release himself from my grasp. His strength when he is like this is too much for me. Tonight, I find the power I need and keep a firm hold, dragging him up the path and into the flat.

Shaking his head with the familiar look of disapproval, Roger walks back to his house completely unaware just how close he came to losing his precious pet.

Locking Jayden in his room, I feel helpless, scared, lost, sick again of feeling this way. Stupidly I'd thought it would all just miraculously become better once I'd left James.

Little did I know I'd be left with a monster even worse.

This problem is too big for me to cope with on my own. Jayden has psychological issues I'm not qualified to deal with, my first thought to drag him back to the monster I escaped from.

That monster I can cope with.

The mini monster in the next room?

He is on another level too evil even for me to understand. Surely James will be able to control him, beat whatever he has inside of him out? Will he even be shocked when I tell him? If Jayden is capable of all this at nearly seven years of age, what will he be capable of doing at twenty-seven? He will get too big and too strong for me to control and then what will I do? I can't, won't leave him, ever, but this problem will get worse if I don't get help soon. Animals won't be the only things that he'll kill.

Walking quickly to the bathroom to wash my arm, dressing it in as many plasters as I can, wincing as the last plaster is put on, I'm reminded how lucky I am to have only come out with a scratch.

I don't have the strength to deal with this alone, and if I'm honest,

I'm afraid of him. I'm afraid he will hurt me again, or even worse kill me, and then who will look after him?

Hurrying to grab everything needed to clean the wardrobe, gloves, rubbish bags, disinfectant, baking soda and air freshener all go into a spare bag, filling up a bucket with boiling hot water and washing detergent making sure it isn't too heavy.

No one else can see what he's done.

They'll send him away and that is something I can't, won't let happen.

Making my way to the garage, burning my legs with hot water a couple of times, I pray it won't take long, tying a blue and white feathered scarf around my nose, crossing myself and entering, freeing another swarm of flies.

Heaving from the smell, questioning if I can do it, I leave the garage door slightly open as legs that want to run the other way force themselves slowly forwards. Dripping some of the water from the bucket onto the concrete, nearly making myself slip, I steady myself, opening the doors, preparing myself for the grisly task ahead.

Maggots crawl up my arms in between retching as I throw the knife and each of the heads in a plastic bag. Grinning at me, their smiles of death dare me to look into their one vacant eye, judging me like so many others, blaming me for their lives ending.

It's my fault.

I gave birth to him and now these poor animals, who didn't have any choice, have become more victims.

I don't want to see them.

I want them gone, destroyed so I don't have to admit what he's done.

Once the heads are gone, I can ignore it all and pretend none of it has happened.

Pulling the last head off the wall, a tiny sausage dog I remember seeing wandering around the streets, has one eye drooping at the corner with what looks like tears coming from it. Mouth pulled into a snarl ready to bite, I imagine it had tried very hard to survive.

Throwing it in the bag with the rest, hundreds of flies land around my eyes, nose, and ears, seeing my scarf has fallen, pulling it back over my nose and mouth again. Dragging the bag full of heads to the edge of the wardrobe, kicking it onto the concrete floor, a loud thud as it lands reminds me how fragile these animals were.

Crack.

Coughing, gulping the putrid air, drowning as my lungs work hard to syphon the combined smells from getting inside my body, I grab the bucket with my good arm and drag it to the edge, mustering all the strength I have, throwing the hot soapy water over the floor, watching the blanket of maggot's squirm. Collecting them, and my vomit with my gloved hands, opening another bag to dispose of them, some feast on my fresh vomit, stopping myself from being sick again as a few crawl up my arm. Flicking them off, squishing them with my foot, I scatter the inside with disinfectant and get on my hands and knees scrubbing the blood, vomit, and liquids off the floor.

Scouring, my guilty tears help clean the floor, gagging from the smell.

Ripping open the baking soda, throwing most of the contents on the wardrobe floor hoping a miracle happens and it will help neutralise the smell, I spray the wardrobe with the air freshener, until the can is empty.

Making sure I've left nothing inside, above me, hidden from sight, I see a tiny box pushed under a loose board, raising my hand to retrieve it.

A box of matches with the name '*The Orchard*' on it are nearly empty. He must've got these from my bag. These are the same box of matches I picked up the day we left James. Throwing them to the ground I don't want to believe my son could be responsible for a family nearly dying.

Please God no. Jumping out to the bag full of heads, the box of used matches is tossed in with them, looking to see if there is anything I can use to help transport them to the bin. An old shopping trolley in the corner looks perfect, running to get it, laying it on its side and using my foot to push the heavy bag inside. Lifting the trolley with my last bit of strength, I lug it to the bin.

I can't believe I'm doing it again.

Whose animals were these?

Where are the rest of their bodies?

Were the families still looking for them?

Was Jayden responsible for lighting the fire above the shop?

Opening the lid, looking around to see if anyone is watching, I throw the heads one by one into another bag that's already open. Gripping the knife, covering it and the heads with other rubbish, flinging the shopping trolley on top, I will never understand why he has done this.

I will never understand why these poor creatures had to suffer.

Was it to make me suffer, to punish me? Does he hate me that much? Will his killing eventually extend to people?

I want to be in the bin with these creatures so I don't have to deal with him anymore. It would be better for me to be dead, too.

Tearing the gloves off my hands, they are no longer a vibrant yellow but now a filthy dull mustard with hints of red. Tossing them in the bin with the scarf around my neck, I don't know why I chose it. It's my favourite. The bucket, scrubbing brush and disinfectant are also tossed in, happy to be rid of them.

My clothes, stained and smelling just as bad as the insides of the wardrobe have to come off. I have to wash the filth and smell of death off me.

My head could easily snap off and float away, detaching from a body so laden with shame and guilt that it can no longer move.

I have failed so badly as a mother, this final act surely right there up at the top.

Would any other mother have done the same?

Spraying the rest of the baking soda over everything, looking up towards the heavens, at least it's collection day tomorrow and the heads will only have to stay inside the bin for one night.

A voice behind makes me jump.

"Sita. Sita, where are you?"

A boy approaching hands me a flyer with a picture of his cat, who, he says, has been missing for weeks. His face is badly deformed, like he has been burnt, diverting my eyes away from him, looking at the flyer. A beautiful black and white cat sits on his lap as he strokes its magnificent fur. It has four white paws and long whiskers with a black patch around one of its eyes that makes it look like a pirate.

"Have you seen my cat? I haven't seen her for weeks. I live just around the block, by the corner shop. My house was the one that nearly burnt down, but it's ok now. I'm Jono, can you let me know if you see her."

His mother runs after him, smiling as she approaches. Absentmindedly placing her hand to her nose, looking at me with the same pain as her son's, her voice cracks, asking the same question about their cat.

Shaking my head from side to side, unable to keep her gaze, her son must be around the same age as Jayden. Was this the family that nearly died?

Nodding, waiting till they are far enough away to release the tears I've been holding in, my hands are wet, listening to them call for their pet.

I hate myself.

I hate my son.

What have I done?

Their cat's head lays in the bin with all the rest. Their beautiful cat is dead because of my son.

My son.

I lied to that family to protect my evil son.

I have to get away from the bin, the heads, the smell. Scrunching up the flyer, tossing it in with the rest of the rubbish, I wipe the tears from my eyes.

I know what has to be done.

Stumbling through the kitchen to the bedrooms, it's too quiet, running to Jayden's room, checking to see if it is still locked. Fetching the key from my pocket, my shaky hand finds the right one and opens his door.

Sitting on his round red rug, waiting, arms folded, he stares straight at me, smiling. In front of him lay several animals' eyes, daring me with his own to come and get them.

He is so hard to love at the moment.

Sometimes I wish my body had just rejected him.

I've seen that smile before on the beast I have to find the courage to return to. Will Jayden's smile be so bright once he realises where I'm taking him?

"You'll wipe that smile off your face soon enough you evil little bastard."

Retrieving his suitcase from underneath his bed, packing it with some of his clothes, he laughs, playing with the eyes.

I don't know who I'm more terrified of.

Him or my husband?

I can't stay here, run the risk of him being reported and taken away from me. Even when he is being like this, I'd rather have him battered and bruised.

Near me.

In some ways I'll have a purpose again.

He will need me.

Checking all the windows, locking his door, leaving him playing with the eyes on his bedroom floor, I step into the shower, letting the scorching hot water beat down on my weary body. Scrubbing all the filth and guilt from my skin, scouring my body twice with soap and a loofah until I'm raw, I scrub the grime from underneath my nails with a brush, making sure all the dirt is gone. The water beats down on my head combining with the steam of tears running down my face.

I won't cry in front of him or let him see me like this.

I won't let him see how much he affects me.

Reaching for my peach shampoo, washing the smell of death off me once, twice, three times.

I don't want any residual smell of the garage on me. Opening a window, allowing the steam to escape, the mirror, now completely steamed over, trickles with condensation as it slowly clears.

I don't recognise the person staring back at me. How have I become so detached from who I am? It's times like these I wish my mother was still here. She would've known what to do. She would've helped me, protected me from the monster I'm going back to.

"Mum, help me please? Wherever you are. I don't know if I have the strength anymore to go on. Please, help me."

Hearing noises from the bedroom, quickly gathering up my soiled clothes with my feet, popping on a new pair of gloves I've found below the sink, I place them in another rubbish bag, shutting away the smell, quickly using my towel to wash the floor before dropping it in the same bag with my clothes. Hastily dressing, walking the few steps to my bedroom, throwing whatever I can into a suitcase, the reality of what is happening and terror of returning to James is overwhelming me; needing something, anything to get me through this.

Running to my bottle of wine, pouring myself a large glass, gulping it back, I don't care that it's only mid-afternoon, I need some Dutch courage for what's ahead.

I'm going to miss my space so much. I really thought moving here would be the start of new beginnings for us.

I really thought we'd be free, at last.

Gulping the last bit of liquid from the bottle, my thoughts aren't helping at all. I have to stay focused. Money? Where is it? I hid it to keep it safe. Grabbing both hands to my head, closing my eyes, "Where? Mum, help me. Where did I leave the money?"

Replaying everything in my mind, I think I know where it is.

Dropping to my knees, poking my head inside the cupboard below the kitchen sink, my bones dig into the tiles beneath as I move soap boxes out of the way, finding not only the money but a few mouse droppings too. Retrieving the plastic carton, washing it before counting how much I have left, it isn't much, only about $200, but it will be enough for a cab and train. The irony of living within miles of my monster husband actually makes me laugh.

Would I have ever been free?

Unlocking Jayden's door, telling him to stand up and follow, he is unnervingly quiet, not taking his eyes off me or the eyes which are still in his hands.

"Leave them on the floor."

Releasing them, they fall to the floor scattering in different directions, taking hold of his shoulders, directing him down the hallway to the bathroom. He can't help looking back at them.

What does he see in them?

Why does he want them so much?

Pushing him into the bathroom, closing the door on them, I make him shower and change clothes, depositing his soiled clothes with my own.

"Now we're just going to clean up the eyes and put everything in the rubbish. We can't let anyone see them. They'll take you away from me if they do."

Using the same rubber gloves, running after his little legs to his room, he screams, thrashing the walls, standing over his precious possessions. Growling, guarding them, daring me to come close, today I don't care.

"I'm not in the mood for this, Jayden. Move away from the eyes. Now!"

Kicking, biting, hitting me, trying with all his might to pick them up, I stand firm, picking each one up, dropping it in with the rest of the filthy clothes. Ripping off my gloves, ignoring his wailing, I seal the bag, looking around one last time, grabbing him and the suitcases, leading him out of his room to phone a cab.

Ten minutes later, a honk outside lets me know it's arrived.

The late afternoon air bites my nose and ears as I lead Jayden, who is wailing, to the waiting car. Throwing the bag full of clothes and eyes in the bin as I pass, I'm happy to be rid of them. Any reminder of what he's done now buried with all the others, I look at my little flat for the last time.

It breaks my heart so much to have to leave, wishing it could've been different.

I wish Jayden could have let it happen.

Closing the door on that chapter, preparing myself for the next, the cab driver picks up on my mood opening the back of his car for our suitcases.

"Don't worry, lady. I'm sure you got a nice place to go now."

If only he knew?

Pushing Jayden in, giving the driver the address, his little eyes widen in terror as he realises where we're going.

People walk towards us, unnerved to see Jono again. Handing me another flyer, his mother smiles at Jayden who smiles back holding up an eye. Quickly grabbing it out of his hand before she bends and squints into the back seat, my heart and head are thumping.

"What you got there? Is it a sweet? What's your name?"

Praying he stays quiet, my prayers are ignored, begging Jono and his mother to leave.

"My name's Jayden, and it's not a sweet, it's an eye. I know you from school, don't I? You're the boy who's melted and scary."

Finding his mouth, my hand tells him to stop, pushing him across to the other side of the car. Jono's mother, I know, senses something is wrong.

"Well if you see our cat please let us know. Jono's out of his mind with worry. C'mon darling, it's really smelly here. Thank goodness the bins are being collected tomorrow." Looking straight ahead, watching Jono and Jayden staring at each other with hate, I clutch the hard eye in my hand, quickly asking the driver to go. Trying my best to smile at Jono's mother, I need to get out before Jayden says something else. Shading my eyes from the afternoon sun, I wave goodbye to her and my old life.

Chapter Twenty-Two

"I can't take you there lady. There's been an accident and the roads are closed off. Better you go by train to the nearest stop and walk."

Asking him to drop me off at the train station, I'm still clutching the eye, opening my hand, staring down at it looking up at me while Jayden growls to get it. Smacking him hard on the leg until he stops, I wonder whose animal was this?

Was it Jono's cat?

The risk going back to James could go two ways. Hospital or sudden death, but what else can I do? Ava will definitely not have us again. I'd have to tell her what Jayden's done - again, not having spoken one word to her since the night Tiddles was killed.

There's only one place I can go.

Half an hour, and lots of heavy traffic later, jumping out, grabbing our suitcases from the driver, the hustle and bustle of the train station distracts me from all the thoughts racing around my head.

Not saying one word the whole journey, we remain silent, standing, watching people come and go. Jayden knows he's pushed me too far this time, proving me right when he doesn't even react when I throw the eye in the bin as we make our way to buy our tickets. Queuing, glancing at the different commuters, all chatting, oblivious to my inner torment, I'm keeping it together as best as I can.

Jayden stares up at me with eyes so soft you'd guess he couldn't even hurt a fly.

"I'm sorry, baby, but there's nothing else I can do."

A heavily pregnant girl I recognise runs past and into the toilet, quickly buying our tickets and rushing after her with Jayden and our suitcases.

Short, low moaning guttural sounds similar to a growling bear comes from one of the cubicles, checking to see if anyone else is in the bathroom, locking the door. Following spots of blood to a closed door, banging it hard.

"Hello, are you alright?"

Moaning longer and deeper, the cubicle door opens and bird-like, deep, hazel-green eyes stare into mine, confused, in obvious pain, pleading for help. Sitting on the edge of the toilet, ready to give birth, she's not coping with what is happening.

Pulling her off the seat, guiding her to the floor and all fours, the baby's head is crowning, supporting it as another contraction comes.

"Breathe, nice and slow, in and out. Breathe. In and out. In and out. That's a good girl."

I remember who she is, hoping we'd meet again, but not like this. She knows me, too.

"Hey, Angel Lady. Are you following me? You see I bought a coat? Arghhh, it hurts. I can feel something. I need to push."

"Mummy, what's wrong with the girl? What's that coming out?"

"Nothing darling. Just go and get the coat over there and put it under the girl and then make sure no one tries to come in the door. Stay at the door. Do that for Mummy, please? Gail isn't it? You need to get to the hospital. It's nearly time."

186

"*No*. Please, Angel Lady, stay with me. I can feel something coming out. I need to push."

Laying the coat underneath her on the floor, telling her to breathe, a tiny face suddenly appears, holding the head to make sure no harm comes to it. Trembling, seeing a perfectly formed little nose, mouth, and eyes, I can't believe what I'm doing.

Screaming, Gail pushes the baby out, sliding into my hands like a small doll as blood and slime covers my hands, arms, and coat underneath, almost dropping it. Laying it on the coat, opening the legs to see what it is, I'm crying.

"It's a girl."

Wiping the mucus gently from around her nose and mouth with tissues from my pocket, she isn't crying.

"Cry, baby. Please cry. Cry, c'mon."

Triggering my own birth anxiety, I need her to make some noise, watching, holding my breath, waiting, eyes locked with Gail's, not blinking.

"Waaaaaaa, waaaaaaa, waaaaaaa."

Exhaling, crying, I scoop the baby up.

"She's got a good pair of lungs on her. Good girl. Aren't you beautiful?"

Turning, Gail lays down on the coat, carefully lifting the baby to her waiting chest as the baby's tiny mouth quivers and she cries and shivers. Listening to the interaction between mother and baby, my heart melts, busying myself with finding something to cover them.

"Shhh, shhh, my baby. Isn't she a beautiful baby, Angel Lady? She's perfect."

Gail is so fragile, so vulnerable, so young. How on earth will she cope? A mere baby herself, is she even capable of looking after a child?

The baby grabs Gail's fingers, watching as mother and daughter look into each other's eyes for the first time. It reminds me of the moment I looked into Jayden's little face when he was born. I imagine the love Gail is feeling right now is very similar to how I felt all those years ago. I can already tell her love is as fierce for her child as was mine.

I feel so privileged, so lucky to have witnessed this miracle. Never in my wildest dreams could I have guessed I'd be helping bring a newborn into the world today. Without warning, tears stream down my face and I go to grab Jayden who, to my shock, is just standing, watching.

"Come to Mummy, Jayden. Come, meet the beautiful baby."

Walking slowly to me, he says nothing.

"She's beautiful, Gail. You did real good. Now we need to get you to a hospital where they can check both of you over to make sure you're ok."

"No. I don't wanna go, Angel Lady. Don't make me go. I know what they'll do. I don't wanna go. Please don't make me go."

Calming her in my gentlest voice, I try to change her mind.

"Gail, the baby needs to be cleaned and looked over by professionals. So do you. The cord needs to be cut. There's lots of things they need to do."

Suddenly, she needs to push again, squeezing the baby so hard, they both scream as the placenta is expelled. The cord is still attached to the baby.

"I'm sorry, baby. Mummy didn't mean to hurt you. Shhh, shhh. You need to cut the cord, lady. In my bag, scissors, a hair clip. Please cut it, let her breathe."

"I can't do that. I'm not a doctor, Gail."

"*Please, Angel Lady,* I can feel something is wrong. You need to save my baby now."

Bang. Bang. Bang.

"Is everything alright in there? We heard a scream. Who's in there? We're going to get security."

Panic.

Our eyes meet.

Shoving Jayden aside, telling him to go stand by the door and guard it, I rush to Gail's bag retrieving the scissors and two hair clips. Jayden, still eerily quiet, watches from the door with threatening eyes, fingers on the handle of the door.

"Don't let anyone in yet, Jayden. I mean it. Do that for the baby. Please?"

Taking his hand away from the handle, he is looking at the baby with something I haven't seen from him before. Could he actually be feeling love?

"Angel Lady?"

Quickly sorting through the bag, what the hell am I doing? It has to be a dream.

Seeing the small bottle of vodka, should I take a swig, looking from the bottle, to Gail, to the baby, to Jayden.

It's too much.

"Angel Lady? Please?"

"I can't do this. I should just let people in."

"No, please, Angel Lady, help me."

My heart, surprisingly, is attached to helping Gail and the baby and it's freaking me out. Why do I feel so attached to them?

Quickly securing the vodka under my arm, I find the hair clips, testing them, panicking as they break in my hand and both springs fall to the floor.

"*No.*"

Throwing them in the mirror, staring into my face, asking myself a million and one questions, they're all mixed into incoherent sentences inside my head.

What should I do?

Gail shouts from the floor.

Jayden watches from the door.

The baby cries.

The room spins.

What should I do? I'm in a panic. What if I do it wrong? What if, what if, what if.

"Oh God, please help. What should I do?"

"Angel Lady. Quick."

Staring at Jayden's feet through the mirror I have an idea, yelling for him to come to me.

"Take off your shoes. Quick."

"Waaaaaaa. Mummy, I'm scared. I want to go."

"Give them to me. *Now*."

Grabbing his feet, yanking off both of his shoes, his little feet kick in protest.

Slap.

I'm in no mood right now for him.

"Now go to the door and make sure nobody comes in."

Quickly untying his shoe laces, opening the vodka, taking a quick swig before submerging them inside, I wait.

Tick, tick, tick, the clock inside my head thumps.

Gail rocks her baby. The poor little thing shakes, freezing, wrapping her in one of Jayden's t-shirts and handing her back to her mum. Retrieving the shoelaces from the bottle, Jayden continues to cry from the door giving me looks like he could kill.

I don't have time to worry about him, I've got to get on with the task at hand.

Tying one of the alcohol sodden laces around the cord closest to the baby's belly button I make sure to secure it tight before tying the other one around the cord a few centimetres up to make sure the blood flow has stopped. The baby whimpers as the lace drips onto some of her exposed skin. Gail wipes it away, soothing her as I grab the scissors. Filthy dirty, I can't cut her cord with them, running to wash them with soap and water, quickly drying them under the dryer. Using a little bit of the vodka to douse the blades, I grab a few pieces of toilet roll to dab some of the alcohol onto them, cleaning the bit of cord I'm going to cut.

Everything is ready.

It's so thick. I should just get help. I don't even know if I'm doing it properly. I'm not qualified to do this. I can't be cutting into a newborn baby's cord.

The blood oozes as the cord detaches from the baby. Gail watches with eagle eyes to make sure I'm doing it properly.

Someone bangs on the door making me jump.

The baby starts crying.

Jayden stands watching.

The blood.

Fixating on the blood, he stands, smiling.

"Is everything alright in there? Are you alright?"

"Do I open the door?"

"No." Both I and Gail yell in unison.

"Angel Lady, I can feel something is wrong. Something's happening inside me. I can feel something moving. What is it?

Gail's stomach moves again like there's another baby in there.

"Please, you gotta take her. Take care of her. I don't want them to take two of them. Please Angel Lady. Help me. Take her away, look after her. I won't tell them anything. Please?"

"No. I can't take your baby? What are you asking me? I can't. I'm on my way back to my husband. I can't take a baby back to him. He'll kill her. I can't. *Can't.*"

She has no idea what she's asking me to do. I can't take the baby. How would I walk out with her without someone seeing? I only came in to see if she was ok. She can't be asking me to do this. She can't.

Without any rational reasoning I open my suitcase and grab a huge tote bag I have packed as well as a warm jumper. Wrapping the baby inside, lining the tote bag with more clothes, I place her inside, covering her with more clothes. Quickly taking an old t-shirt out and wiping up the blood, I wrap the placenta, alcohol, and anything else I've used in it when I've finished. Tossing it into a spare plastic bag, wrapping a scarf around my head, securing my sunglasses to the top before quickly collecting the used shoelaces and washing them and my hands and arms under the sink, I dry them using whatever is left to tie Jayden's shoes. He's not making it easy, kicking me again.

"No. They're dirty."

"Put them on now. Before I slap you."

Grabbing his arm, yanking him to the floor, the laces won't go through the holes. Helping him up, telling him to wait, my whole body feels like I've drunk a hundred espressos, tying the laces to his shoes, telling him to wait by the door while I collect all of our belongings. Nodding to Gail, she holds out her hand for me, running to her and squeezing it hard as another contraction begins.

What's happening.

Not another baby?

Bending down, hugging her close, squeezing her hand again, this time I feel something soft inside. Gazing down, a lock of her hair is in my palm, smelling it, feeling it's softness. This must be the worst thing she's ever had to do.

Could I do what she's doing?

Clutching her head with both hands, looking straight into her eyes, I whisper.

"Don't you worry, I'll look after her for you. I'll love her like she's my own. I'll make sure she never forgets you and knows who you are."

Bang. Bang. Bang.

Hugging her, I don't want to let her go.

"Look after her, Angel Lady. Look after her for me. Tell her I love her."

"I will, I promise."

Standing, patting myself down and grabbing Jayden's hand, I look at Gail one last time before blessing myself and opening the door. People crowd in to help, pushing me aside, concentrating on Gail, who is still on the floor.

The baby suddenly cries from inside the bag.

Roaring, I know Gail is saying goodbye to her baby and distracting everyone, allowing me to grab my suitcases, tote bag and Jayden and leave before anyone has a chance to ask me any questions.

Jayden has the plastic bag with the placenta, crying all the way to the platform.

Sunglasses on, rushing with Jayden to the platform, I hurry him up making sure no one bumps into my precious tote bag. Securing seats for us, thanking all the gods I can for the train not being busy, most of the people are distracted by what is happening in the station toilet; two long minutes later, the train departs. Jayden is so quiet sitting beside me. How must this be for him? He's only a little boy.

The bag moves beneath our feet, picking it up, laying it on my lap. Unfolding the bit of jumper covering her little face, I smile down at her tiny squidgy cheeks as she sucks hard on her left thumb which is acting as a dummy.

What on earth am I going to do with her?

Have I really just walked off with someone else's baby?

What will happen to me if I'm caught?

What will James say?

What is Jayden thinking?

Looking from me to the baby with wide eyes, he takes her tiny finger, locks pinkies together and smiles into her little face with bewilderment. Eyes the colour of the deep-blue sea and hair as black as night, her tiny face makes all sorts of shapes as she sucks on her tiny thumb.

"Look Mummy, her face is dancing."

Smiling, copying her facial movements, he smells her, pats her miniature body with his hands, whispering in her tiny ear.

"I'll look after you. You won't have to put up with anything, especially Dad."

Watching him with her, I know no harm will ever come to her.

This surprise, this child we had no time to prepare for will give us both a new purpose. Mesmerised, totally in love with her, I already can't think of life without her in it.

The trains moving lulls her back to sleep, and already the day's earlier antics are forgotten.

Bang.

Looking behind me, a commotion in the next carriage has people screaming. Hearing another bang a high male voice bellows.

"Where is she?"

Oh God.

Rushing to put the baby back in the bag, I'm too late. Running straight towards me, he stops, staring straight down into my face.

It can't be.

"What do you want? Don't touch me. Don't touch my babies."

Chapter Twenty-Three

Standing on the train, screaming up at Bill, I'm reminded of the night I told him where to go after he demanded I give him the keys to my car. He'd won the car in a game of cards with my husband, James, and had chosen the car rather than the other option, Jayden! He knew others who would have chosen him if they'd won. I'd run to my sister, Ava's, and had asked Bill to give us a lift to the station, never thinking I'd see him again.

Looking up at his thick, fiery hair sticking to his head, he stares down at me, sure he knows I recognise him. What does he want? Has he changed his mind and come to take Jayden?

Trying without luck to block out the commotion around me, what in the hell am I going to do? This morning when I woke up, I poured myself the usual cup of coffee prepared to tackle the day. In a matter of hours my world has turned upside down. Not only have I discovered Jayden has been killing animals again, but I've had to dispose of all the poor creatures' heads, in a bin, outside my flat after cleaning up the grisly scene.

That flat was my safe place, my escape.

With no other option than to run back to my violent husband,

195

I've now been instrumental in helping a young homeless girl give birth to her baby - on a toilet floor - inside the train station. Not only that, but I now have the baby and I've told her young mother that I'll keep her safe. Is this a dream?

Staring wide eyed up at Bill, he has the look of death in his eyes; I don't know if I'll even make it back to James. I'm terrified, quickly pulling Jayden's to me, praying the baby in my arms stays still until Bill is gone.

Bill's sweaty face is at least half a size bigger than the last time I saw it, huffing, almost purple as he hands me something from inside his pocket. Quickly pulling Jayden into me as I cover the baby with my jumper, I hope Bill hasn't seen her, snatching what he's offering without even looking at it, not happy with all the attention he's attracting. People are staring but I'm tired and need to sit. I ask him to join me, but he's having none of it.

"Why are you looking at me like that, lady? I was just coming to give you something you left in the car. I've been carrying it around for months hoping I'd see you again. It was just pure luck I saw your kid coming out of the toilet otherwise I wouldn't have recognised you. You're lucky he's got a face no one could forget. It wasn't easy for me running in these bloody jandals. I ain't gonna hurt you if that's what you're thinking?"

Staring at the wad of rolled-up cash in my hand bobbing around like it has a heartbeat, I'm afraid the anxiousness I'm feeling is showing, suddenly taken off guard by my moving jumper. Before Bill sees, I quickly hand the money to Jayden and put the baby back in my bag, placing it behind me on the seat where Bill can't see it. He's still looking at me, waiting for me to answer.

Staring at the money in Jayden's hand, I don't remember having anywhere near this much the night I ran from James. Did I drop it? Luckily, Jayden breaks the silence.

"Mummy, it's that ugly lady again. What does she want?"

Glaring down at him, Bill rocks from side to side in his jandals, the sweat dribbling down the sides of his filthy fat face.

"Nice to see your kid is still the same. Listen, lady, if you want to know, I felt guilty about taking your car. Now I can see I shouldn't have bloody bothered. I should tell Jimmy I've seen you, but I won't. He'd be fucking pissed. You don't want to know what he said after I told him I gave you a lift to the station. My advice? Use the money and get the fuck out of the country, fast."

Patting Jayden's head harder than he should, the train stops and Bill jumps off, watching him as it departs. Poking his tongue out, Jayden blows a raspberry while I take the money out of his hand and stare at it, contemplating whether I should just jump off the train and go to the airport and leave on the next plane to anywhere?

How can I?

I'll bring more attention to myself if I do, and I don't have anything for the baby. Not even clothes. I can't do anything until she is legally mine. There's no other option. I have to go back to Jame's. Ava won't have us again after what Jayden did to her beautiful cat, Tiddle's. No animal deserved to be killed like she had. Going back to James will have risks, but they are risks I have to take.

Hugging Jayden to me, watching Bill until he is just a dot, I pray to God my plan will work.

To be continued...

Acknowledgments

For my partner, Andy, who has supported and listened to, sometimes under duress, all the re-edits of the book. I know it wasn't your genre of book, and you struggled at first to get into it, but I'm so grateful you did, and ended up enjoying it! From my heart to yours, thank you for everything you do, for being the calm to my storm when needed, and for always believing in me.

For Charley, my son, who gave me his permission to use his brand name and model one of the characters in the book after himself. You make me so proud every single day, and the amount of joy I get watching your posts. Your support and love is all a mum could want. The world would be a much duller place without you.

For Cameron, my daughter, who is most probably the most patient person on this Earth. You listened, gave me a ton of advice, and supported me throughout the whole journey from start to end. You also designed all the covers for the series. Thank you from the bottom of my heart.

For Keith. A. Pearson, who gave so much of his time to help me in the beginning. I know I was a pain, but you were patient and kind with your words and time. I will never forget how much you helped. Thank you.

For Sian Phillips, my lovely editor. You believed in me from the start, which gave me so much confidence in my writing. I've gained not only an editor, but a friend for life.

For Katarina Naskovski, my cover artist. Thank you for bringing my daughter's visions to life. You were patient and a pleasure to work with.

For Romie Nguyen, my typesetter. Thank you for your vision and for all your help and patience in making this book look so beautiful. Even though I asked you to redo the typeset a number of times, you never complained and just did it which I am incredibly grateful for.

To Reece, Jane, Gill, Aless, Denise, Tracey, Kasia, Katy, Simon, Neil, Siobhan, Paul, Dave, Hayley, Linds, Michael, and so many more friends who patiently listened every time I talked about the book, which was ninety nine percent of the time. Without your undying support and patient ear throughout it all, I would never have finished. I am indeed the luckiest woman in the world.

About the Author

M.A. McNally writes page turning dark suspense in her new novel *Broken*. She has created characters the reader will be invested in from the moment go, inspired by her early fascination with reading anything about serial killers or true-life crime which started in her early teens, living in Wellington, New Zealand. Her earliest wish was to amaze the world with her rock star voice, but as that didn't work out, she finally let go of that dream and decided to focus on another. Writing. She's better at that, just.

Spending her days trying to inspire college students to love English language through writing, it's much harder than she thinks, but she's sure she's getting through to some of them. Early in the morning, sitting at the kitchen table, she grabs an hour to write before work and clicks away on her keyboard while watching the sun say hello.

Currently living in Hampshire, England, she loves to sing (karaoke queen), go to gigs and the odd festival, but most of all she likes to catch up on the latest must see on television with her partner. Oh, and she loves all her kids.

Printed in Dunstable, United Kingdom

65191411R00117